The PLAN

ISABEL MORROW

authorHOUSE®

AuthorHouse™
1663 Liberty Drive
Bloomington, IN 47403
www.authorhouse.com
Phone: 1-800-839-8640

© 2015 Isabel Morrow. All rights reserved.

No part of this book may be reproduced, stored in a retrieval system, or transmitted by any means without the written permission of the author.

Published by AuthorHouse   02/20/2015

ISBN: 978-1-4969-5657-6 (sc)
ISBN: 978-1-4969-5656-9 (hc)
ISBN: 978-1-4969-5655-2 (e)

Library of Congress Control Number: 2014921313

Print information available on the last page.

Any people depicted in stock imagery provided by Thinkstock are models, and such images are being used for illustrative purposes only. Certain stock imagery © Thinkstock.

This book is printed on acid-free paper.

Because of the dynamic nature of the Internet, any web addresses or links contained in this book may have changed since publication and may no longer be valid. The views expressed in this work are solely those of the author and do not necessarily reflect the views of the publisher, and the publisher hereby disclaims any responsibility for them.

Chapter 1

The sun was finally breaking through the clouds giving her the kick-start she needed. She hoped that it would be the beginning of the new life she had privately envisioned.

What was coming gave her an exciting outlook. She was in the twilight of her life, as the magazines say, and everything had seemed to pass her by. She could not remember a really peaceful and happy time in her life other than the children, but now she was going to find it.

Karen had been married to Graham for more than thirty-five years, and somehow it felt hollow. At times, the sadness was overwhelming. What had gone wrong and when?

Graham was always too busy at work. Building the business was his top priority. The first few years of their marriage had been great. They had traveled and enjoyed each other. Karen became pregnant with their son, and two years later, they celebrated the arrival of a daughter.

They became typical parents with baseball, hockey, and ballet. They ran from cold arenas to games and school meetings. It was all a blur, but it was a wonderful time for both of them. Tyler and Carissa grew up, went to a university, and then started their careers. Suddenly Karen found herself alone.

Was that when it all began? Graham was away on business so much, and Karen started to devote her time to her decorating business to fill the void.

Megan, her best friend for years, was her shoulder to cry on. She had always been there. She was the children's godmother and was more like family than a friend. She had held Karen's hand in the bad times and tried to cheer her up when things went wrong. Their relationship would always be there.

Karen wondered if Graham had found someone else. He had become so distant. She had tried everything to put the spark back in their marriage, but nothing seemed to work. She decided to start over. She had even discussed her future with her old friend and lawyer. Paul had reminded her that people change, and getting away might be the break she needed to rethink her situation. She looked at finding happiness as a project; the idea of a new beginning was the motivation she needed.

She checked the flight times to San Francisco again. It was stage one of the journey. She had to be sure that every detail was right—hotel, car rental, and cell phone. *What did people do before them?*

Patience. The checklist was coming together, and she hoped it was the right move. Originally it had been a trip for both of them, but Graham decided he was too busy to leave the office. Her request went unheard as usual.

The taxi was waiting. She gathered her suitcases and hurried to the door. She hoped nothing was forgotten. A strange sense of adventure surrounded her, a wonderful new sensation.

On the plane, Karen read her book. She was not in the mood for idle conversation with anyone. She needed to focus on her journey.

She told Tyler and Cari that she was taking an extended vacation. She made it seem as though she was just getting away for a while.

Tyler would be fine. He had his own life—a wife, children, and an excellent career. Carissa had a boyfriend, but she had not settled down yet. Karen constantly kept in touch with her.

She settled back, closed her eyes, and prepared for the four-hour flight. She had her book, a glass of wine, and her dreams. It was the beginning of a great adventure. In no time, the steward announced they would be landing in ten minutes.

In the terminal, a sense of calm came about. She rented a car and headed for the hotel. It was only four o'clock, and she decided to go for a walk before dinner.

She walked along the boardwalk and thought back to happier times. The city by the sea gave her the assurance and comfort she needed so badly. Everything was falling into place, and she had a positive vibe about her future. Karen had no idea what was in store for her.

San Francisco was just as she remembered. Its charm and elegance had not changed. She had fallen in love with it—and left her heart there—many years earlier.

On Fisherman's Wharf, the cool, salty air hit her face, and she felt alive. Little art stores and food vendors marked the path. There was so much to see and do. It was almost dusk. How long had her walk been? She could feel a slight ache in her legs. It was time to go back.

The hotel was bustling with guests. She made her way through the people, and a sense of adventure swept over her when she remembered the little piano bar on the top of the hotel. After a quick shower and a change of clothes, she decided to go there for a glass of wine.

Sitting in the twilight at the rooftop bar, she watched the lights of the city flicker and come on. It looked like the city was part of the ocean, peaceful and elegant. She slowly finished her wine and thought back to the last time she had been there with Megan. It had been such a good time.

Smiling to herself, she felt as though she was where she belonged. Taking a deep breath, relaxation sunk in. Sipping wine and watching the ocean gave her a sense of peace. Realizing she had a long day ahead of her, she went back to her room.

A feeling that she wasn't alone came over her. Turning to leave, she saw a man sitting by himself. He was looking out over the city, and every once in a while, he glanced at her.

She smiled and went back in the room. She decided to order room service and relax in the comfort of her new surroundings. She sat by the window and watched the people come and go.

I am so at peace here, she thought. *This is the break I need. It will help me think through the past and revisit my plans for the future.*

Dusk turned into night, and knowing how tired she was, she turned on the television. She settled in to watch the news in a warm, comforting spot.

She made a quick call to Carissa and felt the warmth in her daughter's voice. She felt so lucky to have a strong bond with her daughter.

"I am here, and I love it." Karen said. "This is where I belong."

Laughing, Cari reminded her it was just a vacation. If only she knew what her mother had in mind.

Karen assured her all was fine. They loved shopping, lunches, and idle chatter. Cari was a registered nurse and worked shifts. Her time off was great for getting together and doing whatever they planned.

Karen decided to turn in, and she drifted into a world of relaxed bliss. Dreams and nightmares filled the night. She dreamed of a new life and had nightmares of doubt and frustration. She knew she couldn't run away forever, but she needed the break.

Karen's mother had left her at the age of five and never came back. It had left a marked blemish on her younger life, making her wary and afraid to settle. She was afraid happiness would avoid her. Vowing to never leave her children, Karen stayed in a loveless marriage. Now that they were grown up and capable, it was her turn to find happiness.

Morning came, and the sun caressed her pillow. She showered, dressed, and made her way to the café for breakfast.

As the elevator door opened, the mystery man said, "Good morning."

Karen replied, "Good morning."

During her light breakfast and coffee, she was deep in thought.

A voice beside her asked if she would like company.

Why not? She invited him to join her.

After a brief introduction, she found out that Ronan was there on business. He owned a company in Boulder, Colorado. He was divorced and had no children.

The PLAN

"I am here house hunting." Karen felt like she knew Ronan already.

They chatted about the city and its culture. Karen was intrigued by the conversation, and they arranged to have dinner that evening.

She spent the day shopping, and sightseeing, and even rode a cable car ride to Chinatown. *What an amazing city.* Back at the hotel, she thought about dinner. They were going to meet in the lobby and head out from there. The evening sounded wonderful.

When it was time to get dressed, she did not know where they were going. It was rather difficult to know what to wear, but she chose a little black dress with a colorful jacket to mix it up. She looked in the mirror, and a smile crossed her face. Her new life was emerging.

While getting dressed, thoughts raced through her mind. Was she crazy to meet a stranger for dinner—or was this part of the master plan? *I am going to have a wonderful night and keep a positive frame of mind.*

Ronan was waiting in the lobby. He had made reservations at a cozy little bistro that was rumored to have wonderful food and ambience.

Taking her hand, he whispered, "You look radiant."

Smiling, she felt at ease and confident. It was a new adventure for her.

Dinner was relaxed, and as they chatted, they felt like they had known each other forever. They shared a lot of the same interests. Karen found herself strangely drawn to this handsome, rugged man. They talked about sports, business, and politics, but they didn't get into personal issues.

"I am so glad we met, Karen. You have certainly added an interesting and enjoyable break for me." Ronan smiled and reminded her that they had better head back.

All too soon it was over, and they were walking back to the hotel. The evening had taken on a slight chill, and they headed to the bar in the lobby. The room was basked in dim light, and a piano player in the corner played some old songs. They were drawn to the atmosphere, the music, and the company.

Ronan had an early meeting and explained that he was going to turn in.

Karen felt strangely alone, thinking of all the times Graham had left her for business meetings. *Is this a new beginning—or am I expecting too much too soon?*

She asked the piano player to play a couple of her favorites. This was her trip—her time—and she would make the most of it. Sipping her wine, she looked out at the bustling city and felt a sense of adventure flowing through her body.

Heading for the elevator, she saw Ronan talking to another woman. Why did it matter to her? Why did it even bother her? So what if he told her he had a meeting? After all, they had just met.

The night was long. Sleep was avoiding her. Thoughts about Graham, her marriage, and happiness rushed through her mind. After tossing and turning, she finally dozed off.

In the morning, she stopped in the lobby for coffee and a muffin. She sat down and watched the people. She had always enjoyed watching people and imagining where they were going, who they were, and what their lives were like.

What will I do today? Perhaps a drive to Carmel and a walk along the beach? Should I watch the waves and the never-ending sea? Or I could go shopping. It's my choice.

Chapter 2

She went back to her room and picked up her phone and car keys. The weather was perfect; bright sunshine basked the open road. Her life was taking a new turn.

In Carmel, she wandered through the artsy village. Little stores and art galleries sprang up on every street corner. It was so inviting. The weather was clear and warm. A soft breeze from the ocean made the day perfect. She sat at an outdoor café and thought about her life.

Why can't I just be positive and happy? Thoughts rushed through her mind—the past, the unknown future, and what was left of her family.

The roar of the waves and the lonely calls of the gulls made it an inspirational afternoon. She was about to pick up the tab when she heard a familiar voice asking if he could join her. Her instincts said no, but her heart said yes.

"What you are doing here?" she asked.

"My meeting was about a property in Carmel. We just finished up. Karen, I think you would love it here in Carmel. Have you looked at properties here?"

"No. San Francisco is where I want to be. This will be my getaway."

The energy in the air was electrifying. She turned and watched the waves slapping against the rocks. Listening to the surreal peace, she knew it was only a matter of time before something that she might regret would happen.

A tap on her shoulder brought her back to reality.

"Would you like to go for a walk along the beach?"

She reached for his hand, and they started off across the sand. She wanted to ask him many questions, but she decided to live in the moment and not think about her past or future.

The sun was starting to settle in the western sky, and they headed back to the café.

"I think I better head back to the city," Karen said, not knowing what his reaction might be.

Ronan surprised her by asking if she would like to stay in Carmel for the night. They could have dinner and just relax—with no strings attached.

This could be the perfect opportunity to see what I can find out. Without any hesitation, she agreed.

A quaint little inn overlooking the ocean offered two rooms and a wonderful dining room. She went back into Carmel to pick up some necessities and headed back to the room to get ready.

She had lots of time. A hot bath would be the relaxing tonic she needed. She had picked up some wonderful bath products. She was looking forward to their evening.

Her mind went back to the good times with Graham, but then the cold emptiness and lonely times took their toll and reminded her why she was in California. Stepping out of the bath, reality sunk in. Looking forward to the evening, she put her thoughts aside.

Karen wore a long skirt and a shawl. The colors picked up the blue in her eyes. The skirt was camel with pale blue wavy lines. The blue shawl accented her outfit. Looking in the mirror and sweeping her hair back and up, she was pleased with what she saw. Time had been kind, and the mirror smiled back. Was life about to change? If so, she felt it would be a lot better. This was the answer she needed.

Promptly at eight, the doorbell rang. A chill ran through her. Was it fear or excitement? She would find out.

A walk before dinner sounded like a perfect start to a nice evening. The night was cool, but she wrapped her shawl around her shoulders.

The PLAN

The sounds of the ocean and the million stars that lit the sky made it even better than she had imagined.

"Let me know if you get cold," Ronan said.

Does he care—or is he just being a gentleman?

They were not the only couple to take advantage of the perfect evening. Lots of people were walking along the beach.

Dinner turned out to be perfect. The food, ambience, and the company were more than anticipated. Karen told him about her children and her interior decorating interest. She waited to hear about his life and interests. When dinner was over, they made their way back.

After ordering a bottle of wine, Ronan invited Karen to go back to his room for a drink.

They sat on the balcony and watched the night unfold. His cell phone rang, and he tried to ignore it. They kept talking, but the caller was insistent and kept calling.

Sensing he didn't want to answer in her presence, she blamed a headache and left.

When she closed the door, it rang again. Ronan answered, and he wasn't happy. His voice became louder, and she realized he was heading to the door.

She slipped around the corner as he came out of his room. He looked impatient. *What is going on? Do I even want to know?*

She went to her room. Nothing made sense. She took a quick shower and snuggled under the covers.

In the morning, she called room service for tea and toast. She couldn't handle running into Ronan. She just needed to get back to the city to continue with her plans.

The open coast road was inviting, and finally she was back in the real world. *No more strange men or instances. Stick to the plan, lady.*

Karen decided to get to the business of finding a home instead of inventing situations. At the hotel, she called the Realtor who had offered to help her with the search.

Margaret had a number of places to show her. Karen put the previous days behind and headed out.

The first place was on a steep hill. It didn't disappoint, but Margaret wanted to show her more homes. By late afternoon, Karen decided to call it a day. She thanked Margaret and suggested they meet again in the morning.

Karen just wanted to have a hot bath, a glass of wine, and room service. She sat in front of the television, sipped on good wine, and enjoyed a quiet meal. She thought about why she was there. She needed assurance that what she was planning was the right thing.

The many years of marriage and raising two wonderful children alone had taken a toll on her mentally. After selling her decorating business, she had started to do contract work. It was very lucrative but sporadic. She had a personal bank account that no one knew about. When she sold her business, she had put away enough for a home in her favorite city. She wanted to be far away from Chicago and its snowy winters.

She wondered if it was the right thing or if it was a selfish move. Arguing with herself really wasn't the answer. After a quick call to Carissa, Karen settled down for the night.

Television was boring. She did not understand how people could watch it all day and night. It was never interesting and was often depressing.

She decided to call Graham to let him know how her vacation was going.

He answered brusquely, but his voice softened slightly when he heard her. After chatting aimlessly, they said goodnight.

The telephone woke her up. Tyler had gotten the promotion he had worked so hard for. He worked for the Chicago Cubs and did all their advertising. He also looked after corporate clients. She was so proud of him. After three years of hard work, he had finally been promoted. Another chapter in life had started.

She decided to shower. The hot, pulsing water relaxed her tense body. Her aches and pains magically vanished.

Pulling on some jeans and a warm sweater, she headed out for a brisk morning walk.

The city was slowly coming awake, and people were starting to crowd the sidewalks. Looking around, she remembered why she loved the city so much. Karen had originally decided to try to find happiness with Graham, but when she had mentioned the trip

The PLAN

to California, he was not interested. He explained in no uncertain terms that if he was going to get away from the cold, their condo in Miami would be his first choice.

It wasn't meant to be. This is a new start. Close the door—and open the new one.

They had bought the condo eight years earlier. They originally thought it would be a great new adventure, but after the purchase of a boat and a golf membership, she knew it was going to be the same as Chicago. *Just a warm winter and then a boating and golfing summer, back home, work, and friends—nothing different.*

When she went shopping, he complained. Nothing seemed to matter to him except his life and his plans. She knew she had made the right decision.

She watched people hurrying to work. Everyone was on cell phones? *What can they talk about so early in the morning? I remember the days before we had cell phones.*

Karen had never worried about getting old. For her, age was only a number. She needed to get back to her positive thoughts. She spotted a little coffee shop and realized she would love a coffee.

She felt the same sense of excitement as when she arrived in San Francisco; she chose a cappuccino and a blueberry biscuit. She watched the patrons come and go. Some rushed, and others had friendly chats with the servers. It was the rest she needed and deserved.

The time seemed to fly. After coffee, she went back to Fishermen's Wharf and looked out over the ocean. She realized it was time to meet Margaret and sighed.

She was drawn to a tiny store with an array of unique articles in the window. The sign offered to read tarot cards.

Do I have time? It would be fun. Yes. I can spare an hour.

Interesting old books lined the shelves of the store. While she was checking out titles and authors, a strange sense of belonging came over her. The aroma of spices and oils filled the quaint space. Soft music played, and candles flickered. She felt at peace. She knew she was supposed to be there.

I can't believe I am actually thinking of doing this.

A voice said, "You are very confused and unhappy."

Karen laughed and asked the woman if she read the cards.

The woman took Karen's hand and led her into the back of the store. What she would tell Karen would change her life forever.

I don't believe in this.

The small woman had a hold on her—and not just her hand.

She talked about moments that Karen had locked away and gave her an inspiring look into the future.

Karen felt strange shivers up and down her back. It was all too true, and her position of not believing in that type of nonsense faded with each word.

"You were in a strange and confusing place. You must find the beginning and the life you want so badly. You have nothing to regret about the past, but it is over. The time has come to move on. There are three people in your marriage—and that doesn't work."

Karen knew it was true, but she had put it out of her mind for years. She often wondered if there was someone else. How could this stranger know so much?

Karen remembered canceled dinner plans and lonely nights. *Was there a third party?*

The lady explained that Blake would be left behind when Carissa met a new man and mentioned that Tyler was due for a promotion.

"There is something else," the woman said. She looked into Karen's eyes. "You are looking for a home. The home will not be far from the sea. You will find it. If there is a grandfather clock, you must remember this. The clock will be waiting for you and your new life. The clock is a symbol. You must put the past behind you so you can move forward." The woman reached out and held Karen's hand. "Do as I say." She smiled and ushered Karen to the door.

Karen headed back to the hotel, not sure if she should believe what she had been told. A sense of adventure and trepidation engulfed her body. *Silly me.* She wanted to believe there was a future out there.

Chapter 3

Margaret was waiting in the lobby. They began their second day of looking for Karen's new home, chatting constantly about nothing of importance.

"Karen, I am sure we can find your dream home. In fact, I think I may have found it for you already." Margaret laughed.

Driving up a curving driveway Karen was impressed. The two-story home was out of a magazine. Shrubs and flowers surrounded the house.

Noticing Karen's enthusiasm, Margaret opened the front door.

Karen froze when she saw a grandfather clock with an intricate design on the door. Was the woman right? She had said a number of things, but she was very explicit about buying a property with the clock.

They went through each room, but Karen already knew what she wanted. A sense of warmth ran through her. She felt so much at home. All she needed were the details of the sale.

Margaret informed her that it was below her budget, and they would include the furniture at a reasonable price if she were interested. A lot of it she would keep, and the rest could be given to charity.

Karen asked to have the papers drawn up. She definitely wanted this property.

Margaret would get the papers ready and bring to the hotel for Karen's signature.

Karen breathed a sigh of relief, thanked Margaret, and drove back to the hotel. *It was meant to be.* A feeling of accomplishment and peace came over her again.

By five o'clock, the papers were delivered to Karen's room. They went through the details; the current owners had bought a home in their native Spain and were in a hurry to close the deal.

This is perfect—maybe even too perfect. Karen kept her emotions in check and signed the papers. She called her lawyer and faxed the data to him for his advice.

Assuming all went well, she would own the home in two weeks—just as the mystery lady had predicted. Karen tried not to think about the other parts of the reading. *Is she really this good or just lucky? Time will tell.*

The telephone interrupted her thoughts. Paul told her it was a great deal below market value. He told her to jump at it. Things were falling into place. Finally, there was hope.

Margaret called and told her to wait to see what the vendors would do about the contract to buy the house.

She decided to read a book and relax, but the reading kept coming back to haunt her. *This is nonsense. I've never believed in this.*

Karen thought about how the woman had described the clock. The rest of the reading was puzzling.

The telephone ringing brought her back to reality.

Megan said, "Karen, we need to talk. I am thinking about coming to San Francisco. I think Graham is having an affair."

Karen froze, silence filled the charged air. "Why would you think that." *Her world was slipping away.*

"Shelly and I were out for dinner the other night, and as we were leaving, she ran into an old friend. While I was waiting for her to join me, I noticed Graham and some woman come into the restaurant. From the way the host spoke to them, it certainly was not the first time."

The PLAN

Karen was not sure how she felt, but she was too tired and too depressed to even think anymore. *I am not sure I even care, but pride has a way of smacking you in the face and asking what you are thinking.*

She needed to escape into the sleep world for a few hours. How had she stuck it out for all those years while Graham was enjoying life without her? Was there really someone else?

She awoke to a pounding headache, and called Paul. He listened in silence and told her what needed to be done. He would hire a private detective to be sure Megan was right and would get back to her before the weekend.

Carissa called, and Karen told her she had found a great investment property. Her heart wasn't into the call.

Karen's flight was in six days. She had to get her act together and get back into a positive mental place. Too much had transpired to let herself sink back into the numbness she was so used to.

Margaret called and said, "I have great news. They have accepted your offer, and we can get ready to move on this purchase." Karen gave her Paul's number, and Margaret assured her all would be looked after.

The day was just beginning. It was only ten thirty. Karen decided to go out to some of the great stores. There had to be something to take her mind off of Megan's call.

The card lady had not mentioned Graham or the affair—or had she? The woman had said, "There is something or someone in your life that you have had for a long time that is about to be broken. Someone is going to sabotage it without your knowledge. It will be a powerful moment for you." Was it about Graham?

Karen thought more about the remark, three people in a marriage, what is going on, a feeling of deep despair and anger flowed through her. *I am so tired of all of this.*

Enough is enough. Shopping took her out of the real world. She was glad to have a few hours of frivolous time.

In another store, a voice boomed out, "Karen, where have you been."

Ronan was the last thing she needed right now.

"Hi there. I am just doing some shopping," she said, "and then meeting an old friend for a glass of wine. I'm running late. Perhaps I will see you at the hotel." She rushed down the street, not looking back. The vision of him standing there with a puzzled look was unsettling.

She had a number of messages at the hotel. Paul needed to speak with her about the purchase. Carissa was concerned, saying she sounded strange. Megan was apologizing for sharing the news on the telephone rather than waiting till she got back.

Karen wanted them all to go away. She dug through her purse for her notes from the reading. Was it silly to rely on the card lady and her messages? Karen was contemplating a return visit for more information. *Would that be pushing the envelope?*

So much had happened in the past twenty-four hours. Her emotions were running high, and she needed to think the situation through to get back into a positive frame of mind.

A knock at the door startled her. She was not expecting anyone. "Can I help you?"

"Room service."

Puzzled, she opened the door.

A young man held a tray with a bottle of good wine, a variety of cheeses, biscuits, and a single yellow rose. He smiled and told her he had been instructed to deliver this and to tell her to enjoy her evening. When she asked who sent it, he just smiled and left.

Assuming it was an icebreaker from Ronan, Karen sat down and poured a glass of wine. With the wine and cheese, her positive frame of mind kicked in. It was going to be a new life.

The fog was thick over the city, and after a good sleep, she decided to get a manicure and a spa treatment. It had been two days since she had spoken with Paul about the Graham situation. She was hoping to hear shortly if there was something going on.

Time had a way of taking the bad thoughts and changing them to positive ones. She grabbed a sweater and headed out for a long walk.

On her way to Ghirardelli Square, her cell rang.

"Hello?"

The PLAN

"Hi, Karen. It's Paul. I am not sure how you want to deal with this, but Graham is having an affair. It has been going on for more than five years."

The fog seemed to close in even more as she listened to the details. "I will be home in less than a week. Let's get together to talk," she said.

Time heals all wounds. She wandered around for a few hours, sampling chocolate and watching as the fog lifted. The sun came alive and shone down on the beautiful city, but the heavy feeling in her chest would not leave.

After walking for what seemed like miles, her legs ached. *Perhaps I should change my ticket and go back to Chicago early. What might I find?*

The lobby was bustling because of a convention. There was a line at the check-in area. People were frustrated by the delays in getting to their rooms. She hurried past and got in the elevator.

A couple on the elevator was complaining about the weather and the meeting they were late for with Ronan. *Who are they? Why are they so anxious?* Her mind was working overtime. They didn't seem like business couple, and they seemed nervous.

She needed to get rid of this nonsense. She had to figure out what she was going to do with her life now that there was proof that her marriage was a sham. Karen thought she knew what was transpiring around her, but she couldn't be more mistaken.

Maybe it was time to head back to Chicago. In her room, the phone was ringing.

Margaret said, "Great news, Karen. We can actually close early. The house will be yours by Friday. I will have the keys for you."

Karen had so much to do in so little time. She asked if they could go to the house the next day to see what it needed. Her new life was beginning to take shape, and she was eager to speed it up.

She called Paul to give him the news, and his secretary informed her he was in court. She said he would get back to her as soon as he returned.

Karen decided that she deserved to go out for a celebration dinner. The restaurant was still quiet and had very few people in it. She asked for a window table and ordered her favorite wine. She looked through the menu and settled on salmon. Piano music started. It was finally all coming together. She was content and hopeful.

She headed back to her room, took a shower, and called Carissa. She was on her way to work, and the conversation was short and sweet. Karen told her about the house, and they giggled about what they could do when they used it as a getaway. The poor girl had no idea what her father had done or what her mother was about to do. It would be Karen's last fall in Chicago.

Chapter 4

What had really happened? Confusion sank in. There must have been signs. Had she been that naïve? Had she been too wrapped up in her business and the growing children? No matter what had happened—it was too late to fix.

The evening news was the same old rhetoric, politics, and sadness. There was very little joy or new outlooks. *I don't think I could do the news. Trying to add color or nifty adjectives to describe things probably would not work.*

The fog lifted, and a sense of adventure pulsed through her.

Margaret called and assured her they could go through the house this morning. After dressing for the cool temperatures, she hurried to meet Margaret.

Inside the house, the clock was the focal point. Still in awe, Karen remembered the little lady's description of the beautiful timepiece.

"Margaret, you did a great job finding me the ideal location and home."

Leaving Margaret in the living room to relax and make some calls, Karen started to take an inventory. The former owners had removed their personal belongings and left behind furniture and some linens that could certainly be used in the kitchen.

Karen was making a list of what would be required on a short-term basis; she'd wait till she was there to make major purchases. In the backyard, she watched a tiny bird hovering over a large flower. It was pure peace.

A feeling of contentment came over her, hopefully this was the new beginning she wanted and needed. On the drive back to the hotel, she decided to take a detour and headed to Carmel. It wasn't that far, and the lamps in the little store would be perfect for her new home.

In Carmel, she spotted the quaint store. The sunflowers surrounding the door were so welcoming.

The aroma of fresh coffee filled the tiny room. She accepted a hot mug from the lady and explained what she was looking for. The two lamps, brass and colored glass, were serene and elegant. Karen paid for her purchases and left.

The drive back to the Bay area was uneventful. She locked the purchases in the car after she had parked and headed to the lobby.

She wasn't in the mood to sit in her room, so she went to the café where she sat mulling over the house and imagining where she would put things deep in thought, "Well well well. Who do we have here?" Ronan was leaning on the back of a chair, smiling. He tried to act casually, but all the strange happenings of the past few days were coming back with a vengeance. After a brief chat, his cell rang, and by his demeanor, Karen knew he would be leaving shortly. He apologized and was gone.

Dinner was tasteless, and Karen couldn't stop thinking about her stranger. In her room, the phone was flashing with a message from Graham. He was wondering how her holiday was going.

She didn't even bother calling him. She sent a quick text saying all was well. She did not mention her change of plans. She would go back to Chicago when she was good and ready. She would confront Graham and end the relationship.

Perhaps he needed to know the return date so it didn't put him in a compromising position. She wondered if Graham would be that careless. Her mind was definitely working overtime, and Carissa would laugh at her.

Paul called and said, "Karen, is anything wrong?"

She told him about the early closing and then lapsed into a tirade about Graham and what should be done.

"I think you should come back early, confront him, and ask for a divorce. You know you can't concentrate on your life with this hanging over your head."

He was right. She called the front desk and told them she would be checking out in the morning. She changed flights, packed, and went to sleep.

In the morning, fog blanketed the city. A dull drizzle enveloped the Bay area. It suited her mood. Her flight was delayed for two hours due to fog.

She read her book until an announcement over the loudspeaker made her shake her head in disbelief. *Another delay? At this rate, I won't get back to Chicago until late tonight.*

She called her friend and explained the situation. Megan offered to pick her up so she could spend the night. Thinking about her friend who had lost her husband to a heart attack five years earlier and never wanted anyone else. They had a perfect marriage.

The flight seemed endless, but eventually they touched down. Karen was pleased when she saw Megan waving at her, smiling broadly.

Heading to the parking garage they chatted about the events unfolding! Was her mind playing games? Out of the corner of her eye, Karen spotted Graham's car. He wasn't alone. Karen and Megan stopped and watched speechlessly as he helped a long-legged lady out of his car.

He didn't notice them, and it was easy to see what was going on. Was Graham actually delivering his mistress to the airport? Megan turned around and followed them to the terminal. There was enough of a crowd that they were unnoticed.

The lady went to the booth and picked up her ticket. The assistant told her to have a great time in Florida. *She is going to our condo?* They kissed and Graham left.

"I've changed my mind, Megan. I am going home to find out what the hell is going on."

"Are you sure that is a good idea?" Megan asked.

"I may call you later. I just need to get this done." Karen was furious, but she needed to find out what was happening. Was this an affair? Who was this person going to the condo? Karen felt like she had been kicked in the stomach.

The fact that someone was utilizing their home in Florida seemed so wrong, but what if this was a usual practice? How could he do this? How long had this affair been really going on? She needed a lot of answers.

Rage and disgust swept through her body. She had been deceived and let down. For the past five or six years, she had known something was not quite right. She was oblivious to what it really was and how serious it was.

Graham wasn't home yet, and by the looks of everything, she wasn't expected. Dirty dishes were on the counter. She saw empty Chinese food containers and a list of things to remember to take south.

I can't believe this. Why didn't I see the signs that were so obvious for so long?

Two wine glasses were on the table, and an open bottle of wine was on the counter. It apparently had been a warm good-bye before he took his lady friend to the airport.

His cell phone was on the counter beside the wine. She picked it up. She needed to look at his e-mails. Guilt flowed through her as she read. There were many from Anna: instructions where to meet, when she was working, and what she would bring for dinner. The messages went back forever.

Karen froze when she heard the front door open.

He walked into the kitchen, unaware she was there. He looked at her with an arrogant scowl. "I didn't expect you tonight. You should have let me know you were flying in early,"

She couldn't do this—not now, not tonight. She would say and do all the wrong things. She headed to the bedroom, locked the door, and sat there. She was stunned and hurt.

In the morning, a long hot shower cleared her mind. She dressed and hurried downstairs hoping he was still home. She was ready.

In the kitchen, coffee was brewing. Graham came in from the den and asked if she would like some breakfast. *What game is he playing? Why is he acting like nothing is wrong.*

"No. All I want is a divorce." It was out.

He looked at her in utter shock. "What the hell are you talking about?"

She felt weak, but she knew they needed to talk. "What is going on?"

He looked strange. It was almost as though he knew she knew. As usual, he reverted to his old demeanor. "You are being ridiculous."

Karen realized this was going to be pointless. The next step was to call Paul to set up an appointment.

"You are upset and have no idea what you are doing," Graham said as he left for work.

"We can discuss this later." She needed time. She called Paul and arranged a meeting for that afternoon.

Megan called and Karen explained what was happening.

Karen felt like she was in a trance. She tried to be normal—but was not doing a good job.

In the garage, her cell rang. It was the condo office in Florida. Someone was in the condo. Was she aware?

It was confirmed. She gave them Graham's office number. He could deal with it.

Chapter 5

*H*ell hath no fury like a woman scorned. *You got that right.* Karen was in Paul's office. She was becoming the calm, rational person she knew she was, listening as he explained the state laws regarding divorce. Did she give a damn? *No. I just wanted a fair settlement. Let's get the show on the road. I need this to happen.*

After the meeting, Karen felt free and alive. She called Megan to meet for lunch. "I just want a friendly ear to listen to my rants."

Waiting in the bistro, Karen was happy to see her friend running across the street and waved as she came in.

"Wow. I can't believe you actually did it," Megan said before she had her coat off. "You look so happy now, Karen. Maybe you should have done this years ago."

"I agree. I just want everything over and settled," Karen said.

Her thoughts were so mixed up, and she was unsure about what to expect when Graham got home.

By ten o'clock, Karen realized he wasn't coming home. She locked the house and headed to bed.

The phone rang. Graham's assistant was so apologetic. Graham's flight to Florida was delayed, and he would not be flying out that night. *Was he just leaving without any explanation?*

The PLAN

Calling his cell, she just got his voicemail. She decided to face him prior to his leaving.

Backing the car out of the driveway, she headed for the private airstrip where the company jet would be waiting. As she pulled into the lot, she saw the car by the office. She knew he was there.

A November chill was in the air. What was she going to say or do?

Graham was having a discussion with the company pilot, and he was agitated.

The pilot turned around and said, "Ms. Hollister, I thought you were in Florida. I was just explaining to your husband that conditions are preventing me from flying out tonight. And here you are."

She smiled and thanked him. She took Graham's arm and ushered him to a couch in the corner of the office.

"What the hell game are you playing?" she asked.

Graham looked at her with pure fury. "You are not going to leave me and create a problem for my business," he hissed.

So this is what it is all about. I should have guessed. We all come after the business: Tyler, Carissa, and me. The anger running through her body scared her. Business was the only important thing for him. He always tried to make the children feel like they were number one, but as they grew up and understood, they could see through him too.

Tyler was a lot like his Dad. He had an indifferent streak and ignored problems, assuming they would go away.

Cari had followed her Mother, her emotions ran high and she strived for fairness and honesty! "I don't want you, your business, or anything from it."

He was taken aback.

She felt like she had passed the first of many hurdles. "I understand your flight to Florida has been canceled. Go to a hotel, get a room, and then leave. By the time you get back, I will be gone for good. Stay there as long as you want."

Just get out of my life!

He got up and headed for the door.

She followed him outside. "By the way, I am going to list the house. I will make sure there is enough furniture left for you to furnish an apartment, but there are things I am going to take. My lawyer will be in touch."

He shrugged. "Do what you want," he snapped and drove off.

At home, she shook as she removed her jacket. She locked the house and headed upstairs. It was all happening so fast. She would call Tyler and Carissa in the morning and ask them to come over for dinner. They needed to hear this from her.

She awoke to bright sunshine. It was a good sign. She stretched and got out of bed. It was early, and she decided to go for a run. She circled the block and headed for home. She had a lot to do, and she wanted to get it done. She talked Tyler and Carissa into coming alone to dinner, stressing that it was a private family matter.

The afternoon flew by. She wanted to make a nice dinner and ease them into what was going on.

Both showed up promptly at six and settled in on the couch. Tyler had a beer, and Carissa and her mom had wine. They discussed work and Tyler's wife and the grandchildren. The conversation was strained, and they both kept watching the door, assuming Graham would walk in at any moment.

Karen stood up and broke the news. Carissa was furious, and Tyler was in shock.

"Mother, you always make a lot more out of a simple situation than is necessary," Tyler said.

"Tyler, this has been going on for years. She is at the condo in Florida as we speak, and your father is on his way down there."

Carissa stood up and hugged her. "Mom, it will be okay. You are a tough cookie."

Tyler shrugged and said, "Are we going to eat tonight?"

"Tyler, one day you will understand what is going on, and your attitude needs a serious adjustment."

Holding back the tears and anger, Karen headed to the kitchen. She placed the plates of food on the table. It was unreal.

Tyler started to chat about the Cubs, how he was heading to New York for meetings, what Kennedy was doing at nursery school, and how Ethan was going to be a ballplayer.

The PLAN

Tyler ignored all her comments, and Karen felt like she was in the room by herself. Carissa moved the food around on her plate and listened to him prattle on about nothing,

Tyler said, "Mom, thanks for a great dinner as usual. Everything will be fine. I better get going. I don't want to miss the kids' bedtime." After the usual hug and kiss on the cheek, he was gone.

"I am not sure that this was an evening I ever imagined happening," Karen said. She realized she was on her own. She couldn't ask Carissa to stay with her. They hugged and made plans for the weekend. "Text me when you get home, honey."

In the kitchen, the telephone rang. Margaret had the keys. "When are you coming back?"

"In a few days. I'll give you a definite time tomorrow."

Tears slipped down her cheeks. Here she was after thirty-five years of marriage, alone and confused. Tomorrow would be better. There was no point in going over the past. *Look to the future,* she thought.

Graham and Karen had met thirty-seven years earlier. He was redoing his office after his father retired. He hired her little company to redesign and decorate.

They laughed over colors and choices of furniture. In the end, his office looked great. They started dating, and eighteen months later, they married. From the outside, everything looked perfect. Five years later, Tyler arrived. Two years later, Carissa was welcomed. Things seemed great. She could be the mother she never had, and Graham went along.

Life went on—sports, school, and then university. It all fell into place, but something was missing. She worked every day, looked after the home, and remembered birthdays, sports events, and graduations.

When she looked back, it was a one-woman show. She had let it happen. Graham showed up as requested, but he was always tied up with his business. Tyler got married. Carissa dated. Life was on the right track, but she was wrong.

It had all fallen apart, at least for her, five years earlier. She got an offer to sell her company. At the time, the offer was too good to refuse. She hoped they would travel.

She filled her days with volunteer work, decorating contracts, and volunteering on a couple of boards. She missed the five-day-a-week scenario. When it all started to crumble, she picked up travel brochures and tried to get Graham interested in somewhere different. They bought the condo. Why was it so unsettling?

Looking back, the signs were there, but she had ignored them or just didn't want to believe them.

She sat in the silence of the house, trying to make some sense of life, but all she could feel was that there was a huge empty spot. She needed to find something or someone to fill it.

Tears slipped down her cheeks. Why was this happening at this point in her life? She questioned her years of marriage but promised that she would find peace and happiness.

She felt like a robot as she made a cup of tea and looked at the remnants of her life. *Yuck. This is crazy.*

Karen decided to give Megan a call to bring her up to date on what had transpired. She left a voicemail and took a bath.

She found a flight to San Francisco and made a mental note to call Paul in the morning. Should the house be listed right away or in the spring?

She had a lot to do in the coming days.

Chapter 6

Morning arrived, and still her mind was questioning her. If last night actually happened, it was so strange; it was as though all the plans and dinner were just a dream.

The doorbell rang, bringing her back to reality.

Tyler stood there, "Mom, what the hell is really going on here?"

She was not sure if the anger she heard in his voice was directed at her or his absent father.

"Tyler, come in and sit down. We can talk about this in a civil manner. I don't need you raising your voice."

"Sorry, Mom. I am really confused. Dad and I went to a ball game this fall, and he seemed great and happy—and now you tell me this."

She could see the hurt, and it brought her to tears. The last thing she wanted to do was hurt her children.

She explained the story of the past five years to help him understand her loneliness and sense of despair. They talked for almost an hour.

Tyler finally understood what was happening. He was saddened by it, and they decided to have lunch in the city later in the week. She could also pop in to see the grandchildren.

When he turned to leave, she could see his pain. This was not going to be easy. For someone who rarely saw his father, he was not taking this in his stride.

Graham had always been too busy to get very involved with family. He was always there for holidays, but when she looked back, that was basically the only time they were all together. When Tyler married Jen and moved, it was even less frequent.

Time heals all wounds. She hoped this would ease over time.

Carissa had known for some time that things were not as they seemed. It was not a surprise to her, but the affair would hurt and disgust her. She didn't like that type of news.

Karen really needed to vent and have someone listen. Megan would understand. They decided to meet for coffee. It was good to get away.

On the way to the café, wild thoughts raced through Karen's head. Was a normal life possible?

Megan was saddened and surprised as she listened to the unsettling details. She knew all wasn't well in the family, but it still came as bitter news.

So much had happened over the last twenty-four hours. Karen was definitely troubled by the affair. How long had it been going on? There were so many unanswered questions, and she needed answers. This was her family, and she felt their pain.

Karen called Graham's office, but he had not returned from Florida. He was expected in the morning. She texted him about getting together to discuss their next moves. Within minutes, she had an answer. He would be back that night, and they could meet at the house.

Shortly after seven, the door opened and Graham entered. It was going to be civil and quiet. They sat sitting in the living room with wine. She explained that she needed answers for closure. "Where did we go wrong?"

Graham shrugged. "I guess I was so tied up in work that I never stopped to think about your needs or the children. I knew you were doing a great job of raising them, so I left it to you. I became

The PLAN

involved with so much outside of the home, and I didn't have anyone else. You were too busy with the kids. I just stayed at work."

Is this what I want to hear? To me, it is a jumbled mess of excuses. "Stop the excuses. How long have you been having an affair?"

He bowed his head. He couldn't even look her in the eye. "I have known Anna for about eight years, but we didn't become an item till two years ago—when you became so wrapped up in finding more to do outside the home."

Karen looked at him. "You seem to be blaming me for trying to raise the children with an absent father—and then burying myself in outside interests—only because I had no one to share life with. I want to sell the house. It holds too many memories. I feel it is best."

Graham agreed, and he got up to leave. He reached out, but she couldn't even touch him. She was sickened and exhausted by the whole situation.

It was finally time to put the past and the mess it had created behind her and move on.

In the morning, she called the Realtors and asked them to come over and list the house.

A quick call to Paul's office confirmed he was finally tying up loose ends and would sit down with Graham's attorney in the next week. It was finally coming to an end.

She wandered from room to room, remembering, and trying to decide what she wanted to take with her. She began going through Graham's things. She had some boxes and packed his stuff up. He could come get them whenever. His clothes were neatly packed away.

In Graham's office, something caught her eye. At the back of the desk drawer was a metal container. She slid it out, and it was locked. She was more curious. She went to the kitchen to retrieve a small knife. With a little help, the lid popped open. Inside were letters and pictures.

In a daze, Karen looked at pictures of Graham and Anna. Even eight years earlier, they were much more than friends. The pictures were all dated and mentioned where they were taken. Opening a letter addressed to Graham, the words burned into her:

ISABEL MORROW

*My darling, when are you going to tell her
about us so we can get on with our life?*

She felt sickened and betrayed. He had lied to her face; this was a man she was married to for thirty-five years. The little voice in her head told her to put everything away, but the unanswered questions were there. Did anything in this box have an answer for the lies?

She read more letters. Anna had been out of the country for a year, which was why she was writing. Graham had gone to London years earlier, supposedly on business. It was all becoming much clearer.

The ring of the telephone brought her back to reality.

Carissa wanted to know how she was holding up. There was no need for her to know what had been found and what her father had done. Karen told her she was packing and reminded her if she wanted anything to come over when she was off.

What hurt most was the fact that her marriage had been a sham for years, and she didn't see it. Bored and restless, she had actually contemplated going to a counselor, thinking it was all her.

Karen knew she was not the guilty party. From the contents of the letters, Graham had been uninterested in his marriage for years. Why would he stay in it? She could not understand.

She could see things much more clearly. It was time to get on with life and put the past where it belonged. She closed the box, and it felt like she put a part of her life away.

The tears began. Was it the hurt or the emptiness she felt? She did not understand how this could happen.

She finished the other drawers and made sure the desk was empty. She left Graham a message that his belongings were ready to be picked up. If he didn't want to come over, she could send them.

She saw the rainbow in the sun-drenched sky. Finally the rain had stopped, and once again, she felt alive. Anticipation flowed through her body. What was in the future?

She sent Graham's things to the company apartment in the city, and the last box of memories was gone. The next thing on the agenda was to change the locks.

The PLAN

Karen had to find a way to tell her children about her impending move to California.

She crossed things off her list trying to keep positive.

The locksmith was on his way. Things were progressing well, and it felt good.

Chapter 7

Tyler called to remind her that they were having lunch the next day. He sounded good—not confused or sad—and it made her happy. Meeting in the city would be fun and relaxing. There would be no talk of the situation.

The restaurant was crowded, and Tyler arrived, bent down, and kissed her cheek. "Sorry I was late. Last-minute phone call from a client."

They discussed the menu, the children, and the Cubs. Lunch came and looked wonderful. They ate, ordered coffee, and relaxed.

"I am going to stop by the house to see Kennedy and Ethan." School was out by three, and Jen would have them home. After a quick stop at the store for gifts, she had lots of time.

Turning onto the tree-lined street, she pulled in behind Jen's car. The children were waiting before she got to the door, giggling and jumping around. It made her glad she had come. The warm welcome from Jen was anticipated. Karen had always been happy that Tyler had a good wife and family. She didn't need to worry about him.

They talked about the current situation. Jen was surprised and concerned for the entire family.

The PLAN

After assuring Jen that all would work out for the best, Karen spent some time with the children. She was happy they were too young to be aware of the complications.

After a hug and a kiss from the babies, she was on the way home. In the driveway, she noticed the for sale sign. The Realtor had been over, and it was a done deal. She felt a twinge of sadness, but it quickly left.

Karen made sure the house was perfect for showings. In the kitchen, she turned on the kettle for a nice cup of tea.

She looked at the mail—advertisements, junk mail, and a letter from Margaret. She thought of her new home, but it was so far away from the kids.

The lawyer's office called to remind her of the meeting with both attorneys in a week. Graham would be there, but it was going to be fine. The housing market had picked up, and an offer had already been presented.

Carissa and Tyler had picked up the things they wanted from the house. Everything was falling into place. She was waiting till the house was sold, and then anything that no one wanted would be given to Goodwill. She was sure there would be quite a bit left.

The home was now just a place they lived in. Karen let her mind wander back over the years. Graham never seemed interested in her concerns or problems. He had left her to make the decisions and sort through things.

Megan had been the strong arm. Karen hoped they would not grow apart even after the move to San Francisco. Megan understood Karen's mood swings.

It was only five weeks till Christmas. Karen would have to postpone her trip. She couldn't leave Carissa alone this year. With everything that had transpired, Karen would have to stay.

She would ask Margaret to send the keys, and then she could go when she was ready.

A cheerful voice came on the line and said, "Karen, so good to hear from you. Is everything okay? I promise the keys will be mailed out later today." Another chore on the list ticked off.

Chicago was settling in for a long winter. Karen loved Lincoln Park, but the wet snow and dirty streets made it seem dismal and dirty.

She made a list of what she needed to pick up for Christmas dinner and presents. Her thoughts started coming back. She had always loved that time of year, but now it seemed hollow and empty.

Time was flying. She had so much to do and so little time. The next day, everyone met at the lawyer's office. Karen wished it was all over, but she didn't anticipate any problems.

Karen's life was about to change forever. Looking back, there was so much she didn't see coming. She had always been so busy. Had she really let Graham fall into something that had torn everyone apart?

No amount of thinking, wine, or hot tea had prepared her for this. Thinking back, there were signs. The time Graham went to Florida, he suggested that she should come down in a couple weeks. He would be boating with David, Bryan, and a couple other friends. She found out they weren't there, but at the time, it seemed like there was nothing amiss.

She knew opening that box in the desk was wrong, but she always need proof of the bad things that were happening. The contents definitely made it real; if there were any doubts, they were gone.

Karen kept asking herself why he didn't just leave. Living two lives must have been trying at the best of times. Why did he stay?

Five years earlier, she had realized things were changing. They moved to separate bedrooms. Graham insisted it was his bad back. It ended any romance; why didn't this all make her aware?

Driving to her meeting a storm was in the air. She hoped the snow wasn't a bad omen.

In the boardroom, the smell of oak and leather was actually relaxing. *Now I know why legal fees are so high. They like grand boardrooms.*

Paul's secretary brought coffee and water. Graham walked in with his attorney. They all sat back to hear what the lawyers had to say. The air in the room suddenly felt cold!

Paul told everyone that the house had been sold. The proceeds would be divided between Carissa, Tyler, and Karen. Graham was keeping the condo in Florida, and she had not asked for anything else.

A strange silence fell over the room.

The PLAN

Graham's attorney informed them that the house would be divided between his client and her. Graham had bought the condo as a business expense, and it would remain in his name.

There was no mention of alimony, any other property, the apartment in the city, the boat, or stocks. She just wanted it over and clean. A cold sweat and anger filled her body. *This isn't happening.*

They were told to think the offer over, and get back to them within ten days; after a polite good-bye, they were gone.

Paul said, "Karen, this is war. I am going to have a court order issued to Hollister to give us his books. This is going to scare the hell out of him. We will play this card and see if he changes his mind." He motioned his secretary to get on it right away.

Tired and disappointed, she wanted to run away. She asked him to see what he could do.

She really couldn't believe what had happened. She thought it would be over that day, but it looked like it was just starting.

She decided to go shopping to take her mind off the mess that was unfolding around her.

"Noah, how nice to see you," she said. He was a member of the board at Graham's company.

They decided to have a coffee. They watched people hurry and laugh with arms full of gifts.

Noah said, "I am aware of the divorce. I hope you don't mind me saying this, but you deserve much more than what you got with Graham. He has been having an affair for years."

She was stunned. *Everyone else knew?*

Sensing the hurt, he quickly apologized. "After a board meeting some time earlier, Anna happened to stop in and was waiting for Graham in his office. I walked by and saw the warm embrace. They thought everyone was gone for the day and had let down their guard. No one else knows, as far as I am concerned."

Her day was quickly going downhill. She decided to stop at the gym to dispel all her pent-up anger.

The gym was decorated for the holidays. A quick workout proved to be the tonic needed. A hot shower and a feeling of completion made it all worthwhile. Exercise somehow made her feel upbeat.

~ 37 ~

After the gym, she felt better. She had messages from Carissa, Megan, and Noah. How did he know her number—and why was he calling?

"Hi, Karen. I was worried when you left in such a hurry. Are you okay?"

"I'm fine. I just needed to work out. How did you know my number?"

"It was on the board member list. If we need Graham and can't reach him, you're the alternate."

After thanking him for the coffee, she hung up. Why was everything spinning out of control? Maybe Carissa was right. Karen was becoming so melodramatic and imagining the worst.

She drove home in a storm. She hated winter, she only enjoyed the holidays. She took her packages into the house. She had not bothered to get a Christmas tree.

The house seemed cold and quiet. It knew all their hidden secrets and was saddened by them.

She filled Megan in on the mess of a morning, and they made plans to go shopping. It was better to keep focused.

Kennedy had e-mailed her Christmas list, and Ethan's followed. It was good to know what they wanted. Grandma would make sure they had a wonderful Christmas. Jennifer liked to spend Christmas with her family. Karen had spent Christmas Eve with Tyler's family for years.

Karen wished Carissa had left Moxy with her, the beloved dog, but she wanted company. At the time, Karen didn't mind; now she would welcome the cold nose and nudging to go for long walks.

Should she look for a dog? Better wait and get back to what needed to be done for the holidays.

She found a great tree on the internet and ordered it. She would pick it up when she looked for the grandchildren's presents. It was a start.

On Monday morning, she was making tea when the telephone rang.

Paul said, "I was right. Graham doesn't want anyone looking at the company's books. He even offered to sell the condo in Florida. What do you think?"

The PLAN

She didn't need to think. "Tell him to sell it. And, yes, I want half."

Paul laughed. "I'm on it. I will call you later."

She had never liked the condo—thirty-five stories in the sky, overlooking the ocean. It was cold and uninviting. It was never a place she looked forward to. She only went for Graham, and it was nice to get away from the snow and cold.

She started thinking about the affair—and how much time they spent there, sleeping in their bed and using their things. It didn't seem right.

She would be happy to see it gone. *Let's get through this.* She took her tea to the window seat and watched the snowy world go by.

While checking e-mails, she noticed a client looking for some redecorating. They wondered if she could do it prior to the holidays. That gave her two full weeks and would certainly keep her occupied.

She set up an appointment for the next day. She had to remember to check with Carissa about her holiday schedule at the hospital. They might have to change Christmas dinner dates, which was no problem. They had done it many times before.

Another cup of tea relaxed her. She daydreamed about the other house halfway across the country. She was anxious to get settled in and put her stamp on the house. She felt love and peace when she was there.

It was comforting. As soon as she walked into the foyer, it felt like home. She was going to love living in San Francisco.

The snow finally stopped, her appointment was at eleven. She showered, got dressed, and headed to Kenwood.

Arthur and Lily had a beautiful home. Karen had done all the decorating for them, and each time they decided on a change, they called her.

She listened to Lily's ideas. Karen would have a chance to do some great shopping and meet with the contractor. Lily wanted it done in time for their New Years' Eve dinner party. Time was of the essence.

Looking after the details—and making sure everything fell into place—took her mind off of life.

Carissa and Blake would have Christmas dinner with her on Christmas Day. Karen had everything ready so she could devote her time to relaxing. Tyler and his family would come over for Christmas Eve as usual. The tree was up and looked wonderful.

Megan was leaving town for the holidays, but they made plans for a get together when she returned.

Paul was keeping her in the loop about the condo sale. "Florida property isn't moving quickly. Be patient. The divorce papers are ready to be signed. Can we do it after the holidays?"

She agreed.

Everything she had known was coming to an end, but somehow this door closing was a new beginning, and she intended to make the most of it.

When one door closes another one opens, hopefully this was true!

On Christmas Eve, Carissa, Blake, and Moxy stayed over. They had a fire, and the doorbell rang. Karen assumed it was Tyler and flung open the door.

Graham stood there with gifts in his hands.

"Why are you here?"

"It's Christmas." He sat down and chatted as though all was normal. "Merry Christmas. I just wanted to be here for all of you and spend the evening with the family."

Without hesitation, Karen made him feel welcome. It was not the time or place for a confrontation.

When Tyler and his family arrived, dinner was served. Things were normal. They discussed the weather and the Blackhawks.

Jen decided the children had to get to bed for Santa's arrival. Graham had another coffee and left, wishing them all the best for the holidays.

Carissa and Karen talked by the fire. Blake had turned in, giving the girls some alone time. When they were tired, they headed off to bed.

Christmas morning was picture perfect. There were big, fluffy snowflakes. Karen made coffee, got dressed, and took Moxy out for a quick run. The memory of Graham's strange visit ran through

The PLAN

her mind, but as she had tried to explain to the family, Christmas changes people.

The day drifted by, Blake did his best to entertain them and treat everyone to a great Christmas. At seven, they decided to leave with lots of leftovers. Blake loved turkey and dressing.

The house was quiet, but she had a year to put everything together. Karen decided to make the most of it. Memories flooded back of many other Christmas celebrations. Was it all part of the charade that Graham had played so well? Had she been fooled for years? Did he feel that everything could just go back to normal? Was it just a ploy for the children?

Karen finished her decorating project, and Lily was thrilled with her new dining room. Karen hugged her before she left, wishing them all the best for the upcoming year.

What a wonderful couple they are.

Chapter 8

Karen and Megan decided to do a silly New Year's Eve. She would come over, and they would order Chinese food, drink champagne, and welcome in the New Year. They even picked up a couple of chick flicks to watch.

Megan used her key to get in the house and ordered the food. She got the champagne glasses out and had a fire going. It was so good to have a friend like that.

They watched *The Bridges of Madison County* and *Meet Joe Black*, their two favorites. The food was great, and they heard bells and horns. It was midnight.

Megan was sound asleep. Karen covered her with a blanket. She locked up the house and wandered off to bed.

It was strange to look back. So much had transpired in such a short time. In less than three months, there was the dream home, the divorce, and the selling of the old house. Karen was ready to embark on a new journey.

Sleep evaded her. So much was running through her mind, and she could not get a grip on all that had happened. She kept glancing at the clock. *Please let sleep come.* She just needed time away from reality.

She dozed off, only to be awoken by the bright sunlight pouring through the window.

The PLAN

Downstairs, Megan stirred. Karen slipped into the kitchen to get coffee and rustle together some breakfast.

The aroma of coffee mixed with bacon. They laughed in the kitchen. It was New Year's Day. No stores would be open. Perhaps a movie and dinner? Karen went to have a shower and get dressed. Megan flicked through the television to find some news.

The news was all about what the new year had in store: a better job market and hope for a growing economy. It all seemed so upbeat.

Karen felt a positive surge go through her body. She turned and headed upstairs to get dressed. She was trying to be optimistic. It was a new beginning in so many ways.

"Ready? Let's get out of here."

It was a cold, sunny day. Arriving in the city, they decided to go for a walk, have lunch, and then the movie. Dinner was postponed to another time.

The streets were quiet. Partygoers were probably sleeping the big night off. Until that year, they had always gone out or had friends over. Karen wondered if Graham had returned to Florida for New Year's Eve.

Megan reminded her to stop thinking. They walked for about an hour before they decided that they were cold and hungry. They headed over to a favorite spot, hoping it would be open.

Lunch was great. There was no mention of any drama. She felt so comfortable with Megan. She knew her well and never had to pretend.

New Year's Eve was the movie they had chosen. It looked light, and neither of them wanted to get into a deep or emotional scenario. Armed with popcorn and pop, they settled in for the duration.

Leaving the theater, they were still laughing and comparing notes. They headed to the car, and snow had begun to fall. Karen was glad they were both going their separate ways. She was finally really tired and hoped she could sleep that night.

She laughed when she heard Carissa's message, and Tyler had a left a brief warm wish. She was so lucky to have them.

Opening a bottle of wine, she sat down to plan the upcoming year. She hoped to hear from Paul about the divorce papers. With

~ 43 ~

the house sold, she would soon be ready to hire the movers and get ready to begin her new adventure.

Without much notice, she found herself pouring a third glass of wine. She didn't really drink much till getting married, and lately, she felt she drank too much. Changing her mind, she poured the wine down the sink, put the glass in the dishwasher, and headed upstairs for a good night's sleep.

On January third, it was back to business. She left a message for Paul with his secretary, called a couple of movers to get quotes, and settled in for a day of cleaning and laundry.

Shortly before noon, she received the call she had been patiently waiting for. The papers were signed, but the condo still wasn't sold. She would get half the proceeds and was fine with it.

Late that afternoon, the movers gave her quotes. Things were finally coming together.

She wondered how Graham felt. She was still hurting. Even though she had planned the move, she had hoped something good might come out of a bad situation. After being with him for thirty-five years, she really couldn't imagine life without them. She was starting out alone—halfway across the country, away from everyone. She sighed.

The children had taken the news of their Mother's move in stride, so hopefully all would be fine.

The telephone rang. Margaret wanted to know when she was going to be down. She decided she might drive. It was a long way, and she would have to check the road conditions.

Karen told her she would be leaving in the next couple of weeks and would confirm dates as soon as she knew them.

She was starting to feel the excitement. She hoped it would all work out.

She checked the long-range weather forecast, and it looked pretty good. She could always stay over in little towns on her way if need be. She had to stay at least a couple of nights on the way.

Should she be lucky enough to have good weather, she planned on at least three days. If not, she wasn't on anyone's schedule and could always rearrange times.

The PLAN

Megan and Carissa wanted her to fly and have the car shipped, but the thought of the drive would be relaxing. As long as she missed any storms, things would be fine. She mapped out the route, checking on hotels and quaint dining spots. It could be fun.

She spread out maps on the table and checked out hotels on the Internet. She was certainly busy.

The telephone broke the silence. Paul was on the other end. Graham had not had any luck selling the condo. His lawyer asked if she would extend the waiting period another three months. Karen did not see any problem and agreed. What was two or three months? She wasn't counting on the money.

Looking carefully at the map, she noticed the route went into Nevada. *Stop in Vegas or bypass it? Let me think about that.*

The day passed quickly. She made dinner, watched some television, and planned an early night.

There was a knock at the door. *Who would be coming over this late?*

Graham was standing there.

She invited him in and asked what he was doing there.

"I think we need to talk," he said.

She made a tea, and they sat down in the kitchen.

He didn't even take his coat off. *What was going on?*

"Karen, I want you to know I really didn't plan any of this. I met Anna while she was doing some ad campaigns for the company about ten years ago, and somehow things changed at home. I am not excusing what I did, but you need to know I am so sorry."

Karen felt he was trying to put the blame on her shoulders. He had always made a habit of avoiding involving himself in their marriage problems. Why was he telling her this? She felt uncomfortable in his presence. She was not sure why, but she really wanted him to go.

Graham had to get to the office. He needed to see her before she left for California.

He finally stood up and walked to the door. She thanked him and he walked into the dark night.

When she made her plans in October, she had been so sure she knew what she was doing. After all, Karen had felt alone for years.

Why was she having these feelings? She called Megan and told her what had just transpired.

Megan said, "He is feeling guilty." Maybe she was right.

"Graham is just trying to make you feel unsure. If he was having second thoughts, he would get rid of his excess baggage."

Karen needed to hear it from an unbiased side. Megan had never taken sides in the matter.

She went to bed with a pounding headache. Why can't this just be over? Why am I having all these confusing thoughts?

Morning came, and after a quick coffee, she decided to do something to occupy her body and mind. She headed to the gym. A good workout was what was needed to get herself back in line. The cold, sunny day made it perfect for a brisk walk. It was only a couple of blocks, and she would have time to clear her head and heart.

The gym was crowded, but it felt like a home away from home. She knew a number of the trainers and a few of the regular customers. After an hour of pushing herself to the limit, she decided on a sauna and shower.

Bundling up in her winter gear, she headed home. The sun was setting in the western sky. It got dark so early in the winter; the day had certainly turned colder. She was glad to round the block and see her house.

Opening the door, she smiled. The fireplace gave off a warm, inviting aroma of cedar. It was time for a tea and a reality check.

In the past ten years, things had started to spiral out of control. Tyler got married. Carissa graduated. Was she that oblivious to her marriage? Was it his way of making her feel guilty?

The telephone brought her back to reality. Megan wanted to know if she would like to go out for dinner.

It sounded like a great idea. Karen needed to get away to relax and enjoy the company of her friend. She headed upstairs to get ready. Confusing thoughts ran through her mind. *Damn him.*

She decided not to discuss her depressing life. *Let's just have fun*, she thought.

"Ready for our night on the town?" She gave her friend a big hug.

The PLAN

They headed to the city to enjoy their evening together. There was lightness about the impending evening, and it held appeal for both of them.

They walked though the parking lot and realized shoes should not have been an option. There was too much snow.

In the warm, dimly lit restaurant, the aromas were welcoming. They ordered wine. They looked at the menu and made their choices.

Karen asked Megan if she would consider coming to California for a long visit.

Meg mentioned that her elderly parents were in Illinois.

Karen was saddened but understood. Her parents had died a long time ago. She had never been close to Graham's parents, and they were gone now too. Other than friends, she had no one to stay for. Tyler and Carissa would visit often. She knew that. Karen would fly back for special occasions.

They enjoyed the meal and ordered cheesecake to share. They were getting ready to leave when a group of businessmen walked in. Karen was startled to see Graham as part of the entourage. Without acknowledging anyone, they left.

Megan never mentioned the abrupt departure. It was best left alone.

After dropping Megan off, she headed home. *What is happening around me?* Things were unfolding on a minute-by-minute basis. What would happen next? Why was she finding all this out now?

Karen finished packing and waited for the movers to leave. The house seemed cold and empty. Everything was gone. Once they were finished, she locked the door, said good-bye, and headed to Carissa's house for her last night in Chicago.

The morning was bright and sunny. Having checked the weather, she was comfortable that everything would be fine. After tears and lots of hugs, she said good-bye to Cari and left for her new beginning.

She told Margaret that she would be in the Bay Area by Friday. She had four days. If she did incur bad weather, she could stop and relax.

On Interstate 80, she headed west toward Iowa. If she could make it farther, great. If not, a good night's rest was in order.

She drove for another three hours. She found herself getting tired and hungry. Off the interstate, there was a quaint inn with a wonderful little dining room. She enjoyed her dinner and headed off to her room to get a good night's sleep.

Chapter 9

She awoke to another cold bright day. She grabbed a coffee and muffin and headed back to the interstate. She hoped to make good time. The trip was actually going better than anticipated. *Just a minute. Don't get too confident.*

The radio was playing old tunes. The time seemed to fly. Energy bars kept her going. She didn't stop till nearing Nebraska. Night was falling, and she left the interstate and headed for the hotel.

She pulled into the parking spot and headed to the front desk. She felt as though she was frozen. The wind was biting, and she was glad to be safe and sound. She was pleased to hear they had room service. She headed to the elevator and the comfort of the room. She entered a cozy little bedroom. The décor was old fashioned and welcoming.

Dinner and a good night's sleep was all she needed!

A sunny day does wonders—even if it is cold and wintery. Coffee in hand, she headed to the car and another day of adventure.

Despite any reservations, it was a real journey. She saw so much of the country. She enjoyed new places and new food. She felt like it was the trip of a lifetime. She was nervous in the beginning about the weather and the roads, but it was fun. Sometimes it was boring—but not too much.

The trip gave her time to think and clear her head. Karen had been unhappy for a long time. She felt as though a big weight had been removed from her body. It was time to move on and find the happiness she needed and deserved.

Sun poured into the car and gave warmth and a feeling of hope and adventure. Checking the GPS, Karen decided to take a side trip to Vegas—just for one night of fun. She arrived just before dinner. Finding a hotel was easy.

She settled into her room and ordered dinner from downstairs. It would give her a chance to check out the shows.

Celine Dion was in town, and Karen liked some of her music. There was also a highly rated Elvis impersonator. She was a big Elvis fan. It might be fun; she booked a seat for the following evening. She enjoyed her dinner and hit the hay.

She awoke to a hot sunny day. It was a welcome difference from the snowy place she had left. She walked through the crowded streets. She did some shopping and watched the hustle and bustle of the people. She walked into a casino and watched the intense interaction, slot machines, and people. *Wow.* She ordered a wine at the bar and relaxed.

She headed back to her hotel. She needed to call her kids and Megan.

Carissa started to giggle when she heard about the Elvis show. "Mom, you were always an Elvis nut."

Tyler was fine and busy at work. Megan wasn't available. *Oh well.* She had done her daily checking in.

The dimly lit concert hall was already filling up with people her age. A couple came to the table and asked if they could join her. With a smile and a sense of relief, she agreed.

They chatted about everything from homes to the weather. They compared notes about Elvis and patiently waited for the familiar intro music that brought the stage to life.

Ed and Marion were from St Paul. They loved Vegas and went every two or three years. They had been married for forty years. *Why do people tell strangers so much personal information?*

The PLAN

The music began. The curtain opened, and Elvis appeared. He could have been a twin. He looked like a young version from the sixties. He wore a black shirt and pants. "Viva Las Vegas" rang out, and the crowd went wild. She felt like she was back in time and at a real Elvis concert. It was awesome. She felt alive for the first time in a long time.

Ed and Marion were into the music. They all had a blast. It ended too quickly. The time flew by. As the curtain closed, she got up to leave.

"Why not join us for a late dinner?" Marion asked.

Karen agreed.

They headed back to the strip, giggling like teenagers. What a great concert. They went to a restaurant that promised good food and fun times.

After exchanging good-byes and promises to meet again, she walked back to the hotel.

She watched the city that never sleeps from her room and thought about the fun evening. The next night, she would be home in San Francisco. Home ... that had a nice ring.

She checked out at six, got coffee, thanked the clerk for the good service, and headed for the door. They brought her car around. She got in and headed for the future.

The drive from Vegas to San Francisco was at least eight hours. She could stop for meals and sightseeing and still be there before dark. Margaret was making sure the house was ready for her. Karen already had the keys. All was good.

Karen made sure all the CDs were ready to go. Elvis was her first choice. On Interstate 80, she cranked up the volume and let him take her to the good life. She felt better already. The time flew by, and it was time to find a place to stop for a break and some lunch.

A sign offered good food and service. It sounded like the ideal place, and she wheeled into the parking lot. She asked the hostess for a quiet corner. She smiled and took her to a little booth with a view.

Studying the menu, she decided on an interesting salad. She ordered and looked out into the garden. The meal was good, and she was back on her way.

Perfect weather and good music—all was well with the world.

San Francisco was 110 miles away. She shivered with anticipation. She would be there soon.

She pulled into her driveway and looked around. This was her new life—a new beginning. What was in store for her?

She walked into the house. Everything looked so cozy and inviting. The movers wouldn't be there till Monday. She would have a chance to check out where things would go. She brought in her luggage and started checking out each room.

She started with the kitchen. She would need to eat. Karen was pleasantly surprised to see that Margaret had arranged a cleaning company. The fridge had enough food in it for a couple of days. Shopping could wait for another day.

She headed to the bedrooms. The master was already made up with fresh sheets. A vase of fresh flowers was on the night table. Margaret had thought of everything.

She called the office to see if she could reach Margaret and offer her thanks.

"You are so welcome," she said. "By the way, I have the extra keys. I may have a decorating contract for you when you settle in."

Hanging up the telephone, she realized things were coming together. In the kitchen, she put on the kettle and looked for tea.

She sat in the living room with her tea and made mental notes of changes. The sun had gone down, and the city was coming alive with lights. She was in love with her new home and new city. Karen felt at ease.

She whipped up a light dinner. She made her calls and locked the doors. She headed upstairs for a hot shower, a good book, and a restful sleep.

Her morning was busy. She made another list of things to do and things to buy. The movers would arrive the next day, and she wanted everything to be ready.

Karen decided to do her grocery shopping. It would be nice to have everything she would need and use at her fingertips. The house in Chicago was a memory she wanted to forget.

The PLAN

Traffic was busy. The fog was lifting, and it promised to be another sunny day. Her spirits were good. In the store, she wandered and checked off her list.

"Welcome to our store," the clerk said.

"I just moved here," Karen replied. "I am sure we will get to know each other. Thanks for the warm welcome." With her bags in hand, she made her way to her car.

She carried the groceries into her house.

A bouncy lady with a broom said, "Hello there. Welcome to the neighborhood. I'm Lynn Ruddick."

They chatted for a few minutes, and Lynn invited Karen over for coffee when she was done unpacking.

The kitchen and the rest of the house were coming together nicely. After deciding she had done enough for the day, Karen decided to head over to the neighbor's house. She picked some flowers from her garden and left.

They sat in Lynn's inviting kitchen. They chatted about the city, what to do, and where the good shops were. Karen was glad they had met. She needed a friend, and perhaps Lynn could be one of many.

Lynn's husband was a doctor. "If you are ever ill, he is right next door."

They discussed their lives. As hard as it was to talk about Graham, she decided to get it over with. There was no point in hiding details of her life.

The break and chat were what she needed, and she felt a sense of belonging and contentment. Life was going to be fine.

She packed away the groceries and found a spot for everything. She settled back to envisioning the house completed.

The next morning, the movers arrived. They were on time and carefully unloaded her belongings. Things were put in place, and a feeling of home was definitely becoming a reality.

Without notice, Margaret showed up with a bottle of wine. She wanted to welcome Karen to the city and her new home. They sat and chatted, and it felt like she had lived there forever.

"By the way, Karen, I have a client who is looking for a decorator. I wanted to pop over and give you her number."

It was great news—a new home and a possible job. It was just what the doctor ordered.

She thanked Margaret and made plans to meet for lunch later that week. She finished arranging the furniture and made a mental note to call Margaret's friend before the day was over.

Finally it looked like home. Everything was in its place. She picked up the phone and dialed the number. A gentle voice answered and Karen explained who she was and what she did.

The lady was thrilled and made an appointment for the next afternoon.

The meeting was in the heart of the city. The rambling townhome was beautiful and located on a quiet tree-lined street. Karen was pleased to see a smiling face open the door and invite her into the elegant foyer.

The rooms to be redone were the den and dining room. Mary explained that she did not have a good decorating sense and needed some help. They laughed about ideas and discussed colors and schemes.

"I would really like to hire you if you are available."

They shook hands, and plans would be delivered within a few days.

It was almost too good to be true—friends, a job, and a new home.

She shared her news with Megan and Carissa. The excitement in her voice gave both callers a needed sense that everything would be fine.

I feel like a new person, Karen thought. *This is what I want: new friends to share good times with, work to give a sense of belonging, and my beloved home. It took a long time to get to this point in my life. I'm going to enjoy it.*

Chapter 10

Karen was busy putting plans together and contacting stores for materials. The decorating job was a great escape from the world she wanted so desperately to leave behind.

A knock at the door interrupted her thoughts.

"Hi there Lynn said, "I can't stay, but I was hoping you could come for dinner tonight."

"I'll be there at seven."

With a nice bottle of wine in hand, Karen made her way to Lynn's front door. She hoped it would be a pleasant evening.

"So glad you came. Come in and meet everyone," the bubbly hostess gushed.

They were all warm and friendly. The evening was light and easy. They were so nice to be with, and hearing she did decorating opened even more opportunities.

The door opened, and in walked a handsome gentleman. He bent down to give Lynn a hug and apologized for being late. She introduced him. It was her brother. He was a lawyer and had been held up in court.

Dinner was delicious. *Good food and great company—what more could you ask for?*

The time was flying. Karen decided it was time to leave. After thanking her host, she quietly slipped out the door. At home, her thoughts went back to the lawyer. He seemed so nice and attentive. What was his story—married or single? *Stop it.*

The day was catching up with her. She was tired, and a good night's sleep sounded perfect. Making her way upstairs, she smiled. It was a great day. She was home at last.

After her morning coffee, Karen decided to take a quick trip into the city to pick up some necessities. It was a beautiful day. She parked the car and went for a long walk.

The two-hour walk passed quickly. It seemed like no time at all. She picked up the things she had to get. She was heading for the car park when a voice asked, "Aren't you in a big a hurry, lady?"

It was Lynn's brother. "Hello, Mark."

"I was just going to grab a quick lunch. Care to join me?"

Lunch proved to be interesting. She found out that being a corporate lawyer was a time-consuming business. He had never had time for marriage or family, and Karen got the distinct impression that he regretted his decision. They talked about life and family. Lynn noticed a faraway look in his eyes when he spoke of family.

All too soon, it was time to get going. Without thinking, Karen asked if he would like to come over for dinner later that week. He readily agreed. She gave him her telephone number.

He smiled and left her with her coffee.

The days flew by. Her decorating assignment was going well, and all seemed at peace with her world.

Friday evening was fast approaching. She was looking forward to dinner with Mark. She invited Lynn and her husband too. It would make for an easier transition. She decided to make a gourmet dinner. After all, it had been a long time since she had done that.

She went to the grocery store and the butcher. It was a fun day. She hurried to the stores to pick up fresh ingredients. She was looking forward to the evening. With a bit of work, it would be a success. She knew it.

The PLAN

Checking the room, she smiled. Fresh flowers and a nice table—it all looked good and inviting. She wondered what the evening would bring.

Wine chilled in the fridge, and the aroma of spices filled the room. One last check, and it looked perfect.

Lynn and Rob arrived. Mark followed shortly. They relaxed and enjoyed the evening.

Karen went to the kitchen to check on dinner.

Lynn came in and said, "I am so glad you invited Mark. He is so involved with work. He rarely takes time out to enjoy life. He seems to be comfortable and having a good time."

Dinner turned out to be excellent. Karen enjoyed the compliments. After dinner, coffee and dessert finished off the perfect meal.

Mark and Rob exchanged stories, and Karen found herself in a strange situation. She had slight feelings for Mark, and the fact that he was the brother of a new friend made it even better.

The evening came to a gradual end. They said good-bye and promised to get together soon. They left Karen to her thoughts and dreams. She was content and hopeful for the future.

Sleep came quickly and peacefully. Dreams were meant to be happy and fulfilling.

Morning arrived, and another new day awaited her. She had coffee and called Carissa and Tyler. All was well, and they missed her a lot. They were both happy. She was content and settled in to her new home.

The Graham situation was never mentioned. *What to do with the rest of the day?*

The doorbell interrupted her thoughts. Lynn asked if she would like to go for a walk.

They chatted as they passed the tree-lined homes. Children were playing and dogs were running with them. All of a sudden, it hit her. She wanted a dog.

"Lynn, I am so glad we met. You have made my transition to a new home and state so comfortable. I have been thinking of getting a dog. Do you think I am crazy?"

Lynn agreed it was a great idea. She even offered to help find one.

A thorough review of the ASPCA and various shelters in the Bay Area resulted in finding three dogs that she was interested in seeing. She wanted to do it on her own.

At the first stop, she listened to the excited barking of many dogs. She explained to the attendant that she was here to meet Clinton, a boxer bulldog mix.

Opening the cage. Clinton looked at her and started wagging his tail. When she bent down to pat him, he jumped back. He was afraid. They told her he had been abused.

Clinton was only a year old and had been in a bad situation. Karen decided without looking any further. She wanted to adopt him and teach him love and caring. They got the paperwork together. She was informed she could pick him up the next day.

She gave him a hug and told him she would be back. He seemed to know; he had let her get close to him.

At home, she felt a sense of contentment. She would have a true companion—someone to take on walks and tell her troubles to. At least he wouldn't argue with her or talk back.

In the morning she went to the shelter. They had everything ready for her.

Clinton was bathed. He had all his shots and was ready for his new adventure. She was afraid he wouldn't like the car. Karen hesitated, but he jumped in the back seat. Laughing, she headed home.

He didn't make a sound as they pulled into the driveway. He raised his head and looked at his new home. She put his leash on. He jumped out of the car and wandered around the property.

He seemed at home. She took him inside and introduced him to his food and water.

He looked up at her, licked her hand, and stood beside her. He was saying, "Thank you." An immediate bond was formed.

Clinton made himself at home. He had a new bed beside Karen's, and he was such good company. When she left to go shopping or work, he would be waiting at the door when she arrived home.

She was putting together the final drawings for her project when the telephone rang.

The PLAN

Mark asked if she would she like to have dinner with him later in the week.

Karen suggested that he come to her house and meet her new family member. She decided on a barbecue. She picked up some steak, fixings, and treats for Clinton and headed home to get everything organized for dinner. A tremor of excitement flowed through her.

Clinton and Mark hit it off right away. Karen was pleased. When workers came to fence in the yard, the dog growled every time.

The evening turned out to be relaxing. Dinner was good, and the company was even better. Mark told her a bit more about his life. He had devoted himself to the legal profession.

She wanted to know more about his personal life, but she decided not to ask personal questions. He would tell her when he was ready.

Lynn and Rob dropped over for coffee and dessert. They were chatting and admiring the newest family member. The dog brought so much joy into her home. Graham had never liked pets. It was a constant battle when she had got Moxy, but that was in the past.

When the night was over and everyone was heading home, Mark kissed her cheek and asked if she would like to do something that weekend.

With a smile, she agreed.

Clinton and Karen headed upstairs for a good night's sleep.

Mark and Karen were spending more time together. Their relationship was still platonic, which was fine with her. She was in no rush to get into that situation.

She took Clinton for a long walk and enjoyed the spring day. Karen's thoughts strayed to Chicago. Though she spoke with the children almost on a daily basis, she missed them so much—and Megan too. She was going to ask Carissa and Blake to come down for a few days. She hoped they could arrange some time off to meet her new friends and family.

She was getting more calls regarding her decorating and was fairly busy. Work always filled the void of not having her family close. Clinton was a big help.

There was a spring fling for the street that the weekend. Karen busied herself with making fancy desserts for the anticipated barbecue. She was settled in her new home and surroundings.

The thoughts of the past many years were always there, but she wanted them to remain in the past and not cloud the future.

Neither Karen nor Mark had delved into their past. It never was an issue, and it didn't come up.

Lynn never offered any details regarding her brother's history.

Chapter 11

Clinton curled up at Karen's feet in the kitchen baking. She offered tidbits to the dog. She laughingly told him he had a taste for goodies.

She checked her e-mail. She was thrilled to see Carissa was coming for a few days. Blake couldn't get time off, which was fine with her. It would be just her and her shopping partner. Best of all, she would be there for the weekend's entertainment.

She picked up Carissa at the airport. They hugged and had so much to talk about. She was really impressed with the city. When they arrived at the house, an excited four-legged critter came bounding out to meet and greet.

After a tour of the house, they sat down to have a good chat and plan the few days Carissa had set aside. She loved the house. She told her mom that it was actually a great move. Tyler had sent his love, and she had new pictures of Kennedy and Ethan. They were growing up so fast.

Tomorrow was the neighborhood event. They decided to have a quiet evening in. Karen made her daughter's favorite dinner. With glasses of wine, they headed for the comfy den to relax and talk.

Carissa didn't have much to say about home. Karen was a smart mother, and no questions were raised. All too soon, it was time to turn in. A good night's sleep was definitely needed after the flight and all the excitement.

On Saturday, Carissa took Clinton for a run while her mom got breakfast organized. They had bacon and eggs and nice strong coffee. Clinton flopped at their feet.

After shopping and lunch at the bistro, it was time to head back for the evening festivities. Bags in hand, they headed for the car. Carissa loved San Francisco. Karen secretly hoped she might consider moving.

They delivered desserts to the park, and Karen introduced her daughter to the neighbors. It was turning out to be a fun night. Mark showed up. He and Carissa had a great chat about life in general. Out of the corner of her eye, she saw a tall, handsome young man heading over to Mark and Carissa. *This could be interesting.*

Karen noticed Mark introducing them. He wandered off to find Lynn and Rob. Karen decided to take off and join Mark and the neighbors.

Mark, Karen, and some of the neighbors were exchanging stories and laughs. Across the way, she saw Carissa and the stranger still deep in conversation. She found out he was one of the young lawyers from Mark's office.

The night drew to an end, and people started wandering off to their homes. She gave Mark a quick hug and went to see if Carissa was ready to head home. She was laughing and talking to the lawyer. *I hope this is a good sign.*

On the way home, they chatted about the evening and how they both had such a nice time. The next day, they would do some sightseeing, have lunch, and shop. It was wonderful having Carissa there. *If only she could stay.*

Carissa had worked at the hospital since graduation and seemed bored with the daily ritual. Even Blake noticed how restless she had become. Not wanting to move, he had suggested going to San Francisco to sort herself out.

The morning was warm and bright. Karen took Clinton for a nice long walk and headed home to get Carissa up. When she arrived at the house, she overheard a conversation on the telephone. She assumed it was Blake. She headed upstairs for a quick shower.

The PLAN

The drive into the city was quiet. Something was bothering her daughter, but she was unsure if she should get into it. The feeling was always in the back of her mind. If there had been any problems, it was really none of her business. If Cari wanted to talk about anything, she would.

She parked near the wharf. She remembered the lady with the cards. *Would it be appropriate to go in there?* They wandered around the little shops. She saw the shop she needed. "Hey, let's go in and have our cards done. It will be a hoot."

Carissa agreed, and in they went.

Sending her daughter in first, she strolled around the tiny store. Karen wondered what was going on in the little room at the back.

The smell of spices and incense brought back memories of her first encounter. She thought of all that had happened since that day.

I hope she helps Cari with her thoughts and future hopes.

Emerging from the back room, Cari had a look of intent feelings on her face. Without a word, the lady invited Karen in. She looked at her and asked if she had been there some time ago.

"Yes."

"You live here now, and you have met someone. I can see peace and love surrounding you, but you have some bridges to cross. Make sure you cross them carefully. You are very skeptical of this, but I am telling you that there is still some cleanup to do regarding your old life before you can be at peace and enjoy true love and happiness. Believe and you will be able to accomplish all that is needed to be done."

She arose, smiled, and said good-bye. She went back into the shop. Karen decided they should head to the restaurant for lunch. It would give them some time to compare their readings.

"Cari, I really don't believe in this, but here I am again."

Karen chose a little bistro that overlooked the water. They ordered and she said, "What did you think of her?"

Her daughter hesitated. "Mom, she described my life and how I was in a state of not knowing what I wanted to do. It was like listening to my own thoughts."

"Go on."

"She told me that I will find someone who is good for me, and she thought I already had. I can't understand that part. I haven't met anyone. Wait. Last night I met Josh. Was that what she meant?"

Their food arrived, and the conversation was put on hold. Karen felt a sense of hope and well-being. The conversation turned to the good food and the ambience. Karen knew the reading was having an impact on her daughter, but she left the situation alone.

They strolled through the scenic area and locked into the little shops. Karen suggested a quick trip to Carmel. The ocean might stir something in Carissa.

They drove along the coast. The salty air in their faces brought everything alive. In Carmel, the mood changed from somber to cheery. Somehow the town had that ability.

They walked along the beach and chatted about life and all it offered. Cari was her prize possession. She loved her more than life itself and would do anything to protect her and help her find love and happiness.

"Mom, things are not going as well as I hoped in Chicago. After being here for a few days, I was wondering if perhaps you would like a roommate for a while."

Karen held her breath. She wanted that more than anything. "Carissa, you are welcome to stay as long as you want. But what about work?"

"I have all kinds of vacation left. I thought I might take a leave of absence and see what I can find here," she said quietly.

"What about your things and Moxy?" Karen asked.

They sat on a bench and talked for a couple of hours about all that was going on and how best to approach the move. Karen suggested that they both fly back and get everything organized together. Carissa wanted some time to think things through.

The drive back to the city proved uneventful, but idle chatter kept it lively and upbeat. If Cari needed time, she could have it.

Karen thought it was a wonderful idea, but they both knew everything had to be worked out in a precise manner so no one would get hurt.

Chapter 12

The days were getting longer, and the sun was around a lot more than usual.

On Carissa's last day, they decided to go out for breakfast. In the café, they chatted about a plan. Although Karen wanted it, she urged her daughter to really think it through and be sure it was what she wanted.

At the airport, they enjoyed their last few moments together. When they heard the boarding announcement, there were hugs, tears, and good-byes. Karen walked aimlessly back to the car. All of a sudden, it hit home how much she missed her children.

After Carissa had been home for a week, she had never mentioned coming back. Karen was concerned about whether she was having second thoughts. Not wanting to push the issue, she decided to book a flight to Chicago. She could go see the grandchildren, have lunch with Tyler, and see what was happening in Megan's life.

She booked her flight and decided not to stay with anyone. She booked a hotel, and the only person she advised of her impending journey was Megan.

She saw Mark on a regular basis, and he filled the void in her life. They kept their relationship light and easy. She could talk to him about anything. When she discussed Carissa, Mark helped her decide to go see what was going on.

Mark generously offered to look after Clinton. He had become quite fond of him, and the feeling was mutual. They even went for walks together while Karen made meals.

On the drive to the airport, thoughts filled her head. *What is going on? Why the change in plans? Am I imaging the worst scenario? Perhaps I am being selfish wanting Cari here. I just want the best for my baby girl.*

The boarding had begun when she arrived. There wasn't time to second-guess herself. She only had enough time to get on the plane and get settled.

She sat down to read and reflect on her upcoming trip. She hoped all was well and it was just a blip in the horizon.

She chatted with the lady beside her.

Megan was excited that she was coming for a visit and had already made plans to go shopping and have lunch.

Departing the plane, she made her way to the car rental booth to pick up her car and headed for the hotel. Once she was settled, she would call Megan. In her room, the view of the city brought back many memories. *Have I made the right decisions? Just get on with your life.*

Megan was thrilled to hear her voice, and they made plans for dinner that evening. Karen wanted to relax and get her thoughts and plans together.

They sat in the restaurant and caught up with each other. It felt like old times, and Karen realized how much she missed Megan and all they had been through together.

Karen decided to bring up Carissa's situation. She told Megan about the events in San Francisco and how she might move back in with Karen.

"Well if she wasn't coming, she would have told you," Megan said.

Karen was distracted, but it became easier when their food arrived.

Dinner was excellent, but the conversation was strained. Karen realized she had too much going on. Until she settled things, she could not enjoy herself.

The PLAN

Megan understood, and after a hug, they went their separate ways.

Karen apologized for her mood. She headed back to the hotel and was going to call Carissa to settle the matter. She needed to know.

She dialed Carissa's number. "Hi, honey. I am in Chicago. I came to see you all."

"Mom, I am so glad to hear you are here. We need to talk."

They made plans to meet at the hotel in the morning. Karen turned down her bed and fell into a sound sleep.

She made a mental note to have a positive attitude with her daughter. She met Carissa in the morning. The restaurant in the hotel offered everything they could imagine for breakfast.

The waiter brought their juice and coffee.

Carissa looked tired and gaunt.

"Well, my dear, what is happening with you?" Karen asked.

"I talked to Blake about taking a break for a month or so. The next day, he told me if I go for a month, I might as well go forever. I am so confused and unhappy. What should I do?"

"You have to do what is best for you."

They went back to the room to chat. Carissa opened up about her relationship with Blake. He was a great guy, but he had no intentions of getting married. This was important to Cari. She wanted to have a family, and her clock was ticking.

"The decision has to be made. You should move on. Please, Carissa. It is time. Your mom is here now."

The day flew by. There was a lot to be done. Cari had to get the leave from work and pack up her belongings before Blake got home from his shift.

Karen was torn. As much as she loved her daughter, she didn't know if this was the way to end a relationship. She picked up her phone and called. No answer. She decided to drive to the house and have another discussion with her daughter.

Carissa was on the floor in tears. She was having second thoughts and was unsure of her exit plan.

"Let's think this through again," Karen said.

"I want this to be the right choice for me, but Blake and I have a long history. I keep thinking I have to tell him I am leaving for good," Carissa explained.

"Well, let's get everything packed. Wait till he gets home, and you two can talk."

They started packing up. Karen took the last suitcase and turned to tell her daughter that she was doing the right thing; she would be at the hotel if needed.

Wandering around Chicago brought back many memories. She definitely understood what her daughter was going through, and she still had lingering moments of doubt herself.

She headed back to the hotel to wait. Shortly after seven, there was a knock at the door. Cari looked broken and alone. They embraced.

"I am so glad it is over, Mom. Moxy is at the house. I will pick him up in the morning. I have decided to drive to San Francisco. Care to join me?"

Karen canceled her flight and went to see the grandkids. Jen told her the children would be home by four. If she went over early, they could have a coffee and chat. Tyler had filled her in about Blake and Cari. Jen worked from home; she had an aspiring accounting business and was picking up new clients on a constant basis.

After ringing the doorbell, the smell of fresh coffee greeted her. A big hug reminded her what she missed being so far away. They sipped coffee and discussed what had transpired in the past few weeks.

Jen was stunned and disappointed by the news. She thought they had the perfect arrangement. The thought of marriage had never crossed her mind. She thought Cari was happy with the arrangement.

Suddenly, the room was filled with shrieks and giggles. It was a welcome relief from the conversation. Ethan and Kennedy were so excited to see Grandma and check out what was in the bags beside her.

The time flew by, and Karen knew it was time to leave. They hugged and promised to visit often. As she left, she felt tears welling up in her eyes.

The PLAN

She left Carissa at the hotel because she needed some time to reflect on her hasty decision. In the room, Cari was sound asleep. It was a good sign; they would have dinner, turn in early, and get ready for the long drive.

In the morning, Karen checked out, and Carissa went to get Moxy. Karen was looking forward to getting back. She missed Mark, and although they had kept in touch, it would be great to see him again—and to hug Clinton and take him for a big walk.

Karen knew all the places to stop so Moxy could run around. The day turned out to be sunny, and a hint of a promising spring was in the air.

"Cari, you must look forward—not back. You haven't severed ties. Look at this as a break to see what is out there for you."

The promise of a new future and the joy of having her daughter with her were wonderful. Carissa hadn't offered to discuss what had happened with Blake. Karen didn't ask any questions.

The trip seemed so much quicker than when Karen drove alone. They took turns driving, which made it a lot faster. The food stops were quicker too.

They stopped at a little inn and took Moxy for a long walk. They ordered food, relaxed, and discussed Carissa's plans for San Francisco.

Karen suggested some time off to relax and look around to see what she might want to do. There were always openings in the field of medicine. That would not be a concern.

They enjoyed their dinner and got ready for bed.

In the morning, they went for a run with Moxy and got back on the interstate. Nevada brought back memories of the Elvis show and her new friends.

Chapter 13

Looking at the GPS, they realized they would be at the California border later that day. They were both excited and anxious to get to the house. They hoped Clinton and Moxy would get along. They had not thought about that situation. *Oh well, that's the last thing we'll worry about.*

They arrived in the city in the afternoon. In the suburbs, Cari commented on the quaint houses. "I am so excited to be here. I know how you felt when you came."

Turning into the drive, Karen felt the same quiver of joy. She was glad to be back in her new world. After unlocking the door, they struggled with luggage and boxes. They laughed and watched Moxy running around the yard.

There was lots of room in the big old home. Finding space for Carissa was not going to be a problem. She settled for a big bedroom with an adjoining sitting room that could be used for an office.

Karen left her to settle in and put her things away. She went to call Mark to let him know he could bring Clinton home. He sounded pleased to hear her voice and insisted he would bring the dog over the next night.

Karen thought about all the questions she wanted to ask Cari, but she knew it would not be a wise or productive discussion. What

The PLAN

had happened between her and Blake after four years would remain untold till she was ready.

They drank tea, laughed about the trip, and watched Moxy. The dog wanted to go to bed—but only if Cari would let him cuddle up with her. He was so spoiled. Moxy won and they all headed to bed.

Spring was always such a hopeful time of year. Everything was starting over and being reborn. It was a perfect scenario.

Mark called to say that he would be over with Clinton and suggested brunch.

Karen agreed and was happy that Cari decided to join them.

He took them to his favorite café. A couple of hours flew by. They had to get back to see how the two new friends were making out. Karen asked if he would like to come over for a barbecue later that day.

When they arrived back at the house, the two furry friends were getting along fine. Once they were alone, Cari asked, "What is the situation with you and Mark?"

Karen stopped to think before she answered. "We are just friends." It basically was the truth. Mark was like an old sweater she never threw out because it made her feel warm and comfy.

They decided to do their own things. Cari went upstairs to arrange her room and unpack. Karen organized dinner. They would take the dogs for a walk later and relax till Mark arrived.

Mark called. He had gone to his office to pick up a file. Josh was working. "I was thinking I might bring him along."

"Great. The more, the merrier."

She was not sure how to approach the addition of Josh. Karen waited till they were on their walk, but Cari seemed pleased.

The evening went really well. Afterward, they said good-bye and promised to get together later.

Cari looked for a medical position in the city, and Karen had a couple of contracts that were keeping her involved in the decorating world. All was well in their lives.

Cari came flying out to the garden with a huge smile. "Mom, I got the job at the clinic! I start on Monday."

"Then we should celebrate."

They headed to the city for a celebration dinner. They were both in wonderful moods. Settling into the quiet booth, they ordered and enjoyed the ambience.

A familiar voice interrupted their conversation. "What a pleasant surprise. Did you move here?" Ronan asked. "Can I sit for a minute?"

Karen nodded and introduced Cari and Ronan.

When he left, the air was electric. Cari said, "Mom, what was that all about?"

Karen explained the strange happenings in the past. She had feelings for the handsome stranger, but she didn't know who he was or what he did. Was he really from Boulder?

"Sometimes you have to take chances—and not be so suspicious," Cari said.

They discussed Cari's new job. She would be the senior nurse for the medical center and have a staff of three to mentor and look after. She was looking forward to starting. It was exactly what she had wanted, and they toasted her new position.

After leaving the restaurant, they decided to go for a walk along Fishermen's Wharf. The evening was warm and welcoming. Watching the boats in the harbor, they daydreamed and laughed about where they could travel. The walk was busy with people, and all too soon, they headed back to the car for the drive home.

"I am so happy that your world is finally falling into place," Karen said. "If only I could get Tyler a job with the Giants, it would be perfect."

Karen thought about the surprise encounter at the restaurant. Ronan had mentioned another business trip. When he returned to his table, she noticed three other men awaiting him.

In the morning, Karen went to the city to check on some material she had ordered for her decorating contract. Cari decided to stay home and make dinner.

Karen headed to the client's home. She needed to get Sheila's final approval. The door opened, and she was welcomed into the elegant townhome. Sheila was thrilled with the swatch of material. The workers were there and already painting. Everything was on schedule.

The PLAN

"I bought this material because it reminded me of you, Sheila. It's elegant and warm."

Karen went back to the store to pick up the rest of the material and have it dropped off with Melissa. The lady who was making the drapes and cushions was moving quickly.

Karen ordered a coffee and a raspberry biscuit. The lunch crowd had gone, and it was quiet and relaxing. She looked at the drawings of Sheila's den and remembered that she had promised to find an antique mirror.

An antique store she liked was within walking distance. Another Time housed beautiful furnishings. She saw the perfect mirror on the wall was. She bought it and gave Sheila's address for delivery.

When she pulled into the driveway, she saw a strange car outside her home. She was pleasantly surprised to see Josh chatting with her daughter in the kitchen.

"Mom, I asked Josh to join us."

Dinner was excellent, and they laughed at some of Josh's legal encounters.

Karen decided to leave the two alone and headed out with the dogs for a long walk.

She was rounding the block when a car pulled up beside her. She was glad she had the dogs. She kept walking, and the car slowly followed her.

"Karen," Ronan said.

She stopped and waited as he pulled over and parked.

"What are you doing here?"

Ronan looked at her longingly. "I have been looking for you for months. You have always been on my mind. Until we ran into each other last week, I had no idea you had moved here. There is so much we need to talk about. Please say we can have dinner this week."

Karen agreed reluctantly and gave him her phone number.

He told her he would make reservations for them.

Heading home, she felt like she was in a daze. *What is he doing here? How did he find me? We do need to talk. It will be interesting. So many questions, so few answers.*

Cari was getting organized for her new career. She was happy and content. Karen decided not to say anything about her chance meeting with Ronan. There was no need to get into a heavy discussion. She would let her daughter enjoy her next adventure.

Karen needed time alone to try to make some sense of her feelings. *Why is he such a pull on my emotions? Almost every time we have been together, we've ended up in questionable circumstances.*

Time was racing. Cari started her new job, and she loved the people and the position. Josh was in the picture more and more. All was well in this new world.

Karen was walking the dogs when her cell rang.

Ronan apologized for the other night and suggested a dinner date for Friday evening.

She agreed to meet him in the city since she would be there on business. It was just a matter of waiting to see how everything went.

Lynn called and said, "How is everything going? Since Cari arrived, I miss seeing you. I understand and am so happy she is here, but let's get together soon."

Karen agreed and headed home with the dogs.

Chapter 14

Friday came almost too fast. Karen had an appointment in the city for two o'clock and dinner was at five. She was unable to concentrate on the client meeting. After they made all the decisions, Karen realized she only had half an hour to meet Ronan.

Arriving early at the restaurant, she went to the restroom to freshen up. At five, Ronan arrived and bent down to kiss her cheek.

They were shown to their table. Everything seemed so normal.

The conversation was light. He was there again on business. He and a group of associates were looking at property between the city and Carmel. They were planning a hotel complex.

"How long will you be here?" she asked.

"I will be in the city for another few days."

The conversation was strained at times. *What is he holding back?*

Karen asked, "What is going on with you? Why are things so strange and complex?"

Ronan leaned back in his chair. "Karen, I don't know what you want me to say. I told you I have a business in Boulder, and I am also an investor. Carmel, for instance. You seem so skeptical of me. I try to get close, and you freeze me out."

"I have been through a lot in the past year. I just want some normal relationships in my life." Was her tortured past interfering with her future? For over thirty five years, she had put her trust in Graham, ignoring the last nine years of signs. The past had left many scars, and she found it hard to trust men anymore. She was always looking for problems—whether they were there or not.

Reaching across the table, she apologized. Her only explanation was the past, and she wanted to leave it alone. Her hand rested on his, and she felt the warmth.

He sighed. "I am so glad you are okay now, Karen."

Dinner turned out to be a pleasant event. Afternoon turned into evening. He suggested they go to a little club; they walked hand in hand down the hilly street, looking forward to the next chapter of their evening.

The club played old music. It was dark and romantic. When they got up to dance, electricity was in the air. He held her close, and she felt as though they were entwined as one.

Ronan walked her back to her car, and as they stood in the shadows, his arm encircled her. He bent to kiss her. She felt like a giddy girl, and it was a wonderful feeling. After the kiss, they passionately held each other. Pulling away, Karen thanked him for dinner and slid into the car. She promised to call him and drove off. She had to get away before her body overtook her mind. Her old feelings for Ronan were back—and stronger than ever.

Cari and Josh were watching a movie. They exchanged greetings, and Karen headed to her room. She turned on the television and watched *Meet Joe Black*.

After the movie, she fell into a deep sleep.

The morning was foggy. Mist was falling on the city and the countryside. She knew the sun would come out soon and burn the fog away, leaving a beautiful sunny start to the weekend.

She made coffee and wondered if she would she hear from him. He had told her to call because he would be going through real estate deals with his associates.

Cari wandered down and sat on a kitchen stool. She asked about the dinner date, and Karen blushed when she spoke about Ronan and dinner. The world was getting better every day.

The PLAN

They decided to take the dogs for a walk and continue their interesting conversation. Many times in the past, Karen had hoped her daughter would find true love and be happy. Could Josh be the one?

Cari seemed so much happier than in Chicago. It was a good start. She and Josh were going to a concert that evening in Oakland. She suggested that Karen invite Ronan over.

Mark called and asked if she had any plans for the weekend. He was the comfortable blanket. Ronan was the unpredictable. She decided to ask Mark for dinner Sunday. She had that night to make her mind up about the unpredictable.

Cari laughed at her mother's predicament. "Now what? Two totally different men?"

They both seemed interested in a relationship—or was Karen just flattering herself?

Chapter 15

Josh arrived and waited for Carissa.

Karen excused herself and called Ronan's cell. His gruff hello turned soft when he heard her voice. "I am so glad you called," he said.

She invited him over for a quiet dinner. He would be there by seven.

She stared at the clock and thought of the card reader. Smiling, she headed back to the kitchen to make sure Josh was comfortable.

Cari and her date left. Karen decided to make a simple romantic dinner. They would eat on the back deck. The smell of the flowers and the surroundings made it a perfect choice.

In the market, she ran into Lynn and Rob. They were off to see friends and were picking up dessert and wine.

"We haven't seen much of you lately." Lynn commented. "We miss you."

Karen explained how busy she had been since Cari arrived. They made plans for lunch, and Mark didn't come up.

Karen was excited and hoped the evening didn't disappoint. *I want this evening to be special, but I can't expect too much.*

The kitchen smelled wonderful. Spices wafted through the air. Everything was coming together. She set the little table on the deck with candles. After a thorough examination of the plates and cutlery, she went inside to wait. *Am I being silly to feel this way? Why am I so concerned with perfection?*

Promptly at seven, the doorbell chimed. Apprehension pulsed through her body. He brought a bouquet of spring flowers and a bottle of wine.

Karen welcomed him into her home.

"You have a lovely home,. The personal touches are definitely you."

They had a glass of wine before dinner. The talk was casual, and Ronan told her about Colorado and his business. There was no mention of anything that would raise red flags for her.

Dinner was relaxing, and their constant banter was fun. The evening was going well. He helped her take the dishes to the kitchen. She made coffee and left him to wander outside. She felt a familiar tug at her heart.

He explained that he had to go back to Colorado in the morning and excused himself. He bent down and kissed her.

She wanted it to go on, but he smiled and told her would call her when he got back in a couple weeks. They made plans to meet. After another quick kiss, he headed to his car. Karen felt an apprehensive chill go through her. *Why do I have these moments?*

She curled up on the couch to think over the past few hours. Sleep overtook her. The next day, Mark was coming for a barbeque.

Her good night's sleep made her see the world in a more positive manner. She sat on the deck and watched the dogs play. She felt everything was going to work out. The sun was burning off the fog. It would be a great day.

Cari and Josh brought warm bagels and stories of their evening in Oakland.

Karen laughed with them. It was so good to have them around. "I was planning to have Mark over for a barbecue tonight. Are you two busy?"

With big smiles, they agreed. They offered to cook and headed to the market for their dinner ingredients. They told her to sit back and relax.

Karen decided not to discuss her dinner with Ronan. Time would decide if they would discuss their romantic endeavors.

She took the dogs for a walk. Moxy and Clinton were good company. They seemed to know her thoughts were elsewhere. They tugged at their leashes to get her attention.

The neighborhood was coming awake. Children were laughing, birds were singing, and the sun was burning through the mist. She couldn't get her mind off the previous evening. *Why am I so hesitant about Ronan?*

"Hi, Karen. How is your day," Sarah called from across the street.

The dogs were tired and panting as they rounded the corner to go home. It had been a good walk. She had time to think, reflect, and enjoy. The neighbors waving and saying hello added to her perfect day.

Spring was turning into summer. Cari and Josh were an item. Mark was still part of Karen's life. Ronan faded into the background. She rarely heard from him.

The peace in her life was welcoming; she spoke with Tyler and his family on a weekly basis. She invited them down for a vacation on summer break.

Megan had been down for a visit. Everything in her life was falling into a place.

Karen was busy with her decorating. Referrals were coming in from all sources. It kept her busy, and being busy was good. She knew that not working was a curse.

Cari was having a glass of wine on the deck, deep in thought.

"Am I interrupting?"

"Josh asked me to move in with him. I don't know what to do."

"Just follow your heart. I really like him. He has a good job. You are settled now. What can it hurt? I am here if you ever need anything."

Cari gave her mom a hug, and they headed into the house.

Karen said, "Grab the moment. Enjoy it, and give life a chance to bring you happiness." She would miss having Cari around, but it was time she found her niche.

The PLAN

"I am so glad you are okay with this, Mom. I was concerned that you might feel alone, and I don't want that to happen."

"I will be fine. I have lots of friends, and you are going to be here in the city. We will still do our shopping and have lunches."

Chapter 16

Mark called to see if Karen would join him at a cocktail party for one of his clients. Needing to have a change, she agreed.

Her reflection in the mirror told her she didn't look her age, which was a great feeling. She took pride in her appearance and looked after herself. She had told the children that age didn't matter as long as you look and feel younger than you are. She had certainly accomplished that.

A long, hot shower helped her feel alive and ready for the evening. She decided on a flattering outfit. She wore a long skirt, a matching jacket, and a colorful scarf.

Mark greeted her on the fifteenth floor of Martin Industries. "You look beautiful," he whispered as his lips brushed her cheek.

He made her feel so welcome. He was such a good person. How could she not have romantic feelings for him?

He introduced her to various clients and connections. He held her hand and made sure she felt needed and important. He always took the time to let her know how special she was.

Her second thoughts about their relationship caused her confusion and pain. She always felt safe and warm with Mark. Was that not enough? The past was haunting her and giving her doubts.

As she mingled, she felt Mark's eyes on her. He wanted her to enjoy his life—and he seemed to want her to be part of it.

He reminded her of her previous life. She had always felt safe with Graham. She realized the problem was her connection with her ex-husband. *What should I do?*

Mark asked if she would like to go for a late bite to eat. She was overwhelmed by her feelings and decided to take a rain check. He walked her to the car, brushed her cheek with his lips, and said good night.

Her mind was whirling with thoughts of Mark and the past. She couldn't handle it all right then. She needed time—and she needed to see Ronan. Her mind was racing. She needed to let go of the past and get on with her new life.

Cari was not home, and the house was quiet. It would be lonely when she moved out, Karen was happy with her decision. *Get on with your life.*

Moxy and Clinton were waiting patiently for a walk. It would tire all three of them. They walked for almost an hour. She went to bed. Whatever was on her mind would have to wait for another day.

Cari would start moving her things on her day off. Karen already felt lonely. They both decided that Moxy and Clinton would stay together; after all, they were a lot of company for each other and Karen.

Karen looked at fabrics online. Her thoughts went to Boulder and Ronan's company. She decided to look it up to see what it was all about. The search engine brought some interesting results. The company supplied building materials to large developers. That answered the building in Carmel question. A cold chill went through her when she looked at the board members. There were three women, but one had the same last name. A sister or the wife?

Other searches brought up nothing. Her apprehension was so strong, and she had to find out. She picked up the phone and called Paul. Karen asked for the name of the private detective.

She made up an excuse that an old friend needed some assistance. She thanked Paul and promised to keep in touch. She hung up and called David O'Leary. She told him she was contemplating doing some business in Boulder with Ronan's company and wanted some background about the owner.

"Not a problem, Karen. Give me a couple of days, and I will get back to you."

She felt a breath of relief. She would never be fooled by a man again.

Ronan called, but she let it go to voicemail. He was still in Boulder, and she knew she wouldn't have to face him for some time.

Cari and Josh came to pick up her necessities. They both seemed happy, which made Karen feel better. At least her daughter was moving forward.

She kept herself busy for several days—lunch with Margaret, helping Cari move, and the long walks with her doggies—but nights were a different matter. The evenings dragged. She decided to ask Mark over for dinner.

They watched the dogs romping around and loving the summer evening. They chatted about life, work and decorating opportunities.

Karen heard the telephone. Since it was late, she ignored it.

Mark helped her clean up, thanked her for a lovely evening, and headed to his car.

She finished in the kitchen and checked the message.

David would be sending an e-mail about her inquiry. *Should I dare look at the computer?*

Karen read the e-mail from David. The company was very profitable, but it did have some questionable connections. Ronan and his wife of twenty years managed it very well. Ronan's wife's family owned business. He had run the company for fifteen years. He and Marinna had two boys from a previous marriage. They were both in college.

This sounded like her past. Ronan was just another man trying to find life in another city with someone new. She wondered if his wife saw the signs.

She looked back on her life. Was she so wrapped up in the children that she missed the signs when Graham was cheating? When she decided to move on and make a new life, why was it crumbling around her?

The PLAN

Time stood still. Why was this happening? Why had he lied? Karen felt like a failure. First there was Graham—and now she had feelings for another liar and a cheat. *What is wrong here?*

She reread the e-mail. It was all there. She hadn't imagined any of it. Karen didn't want anyone to know how foolish she had been. The mysterious phone calls, canceled plans, and early nights all made sense.

She felt the burn of tears as she remembered her thoughts and feelings. She was glad she had not found out later. A bitter lesson had been learned.

Morning brought a dull rain that echoed the feelings in her body. She tried to tell herself she was strong and that she would get through this. Why was her world falling apart? Ten years earlier, her marriage to Graham had not been all sunshine and roses. Since the children were not ready to go on their own, she stayed.

Now she had made the major move to a new city. It was a mess. Tears welled up in her eyes. She knew she had to go on and make the life she wanted so much. *Is being happy that hard?*

The past haunted her. Karen wondered if she needed professional help—or was it about giving herself time to heal?

A call from Megan interrupted her thoughts. She was planning a trip. What a perfect time. Karen hoped it would be a turning point in her life.

Chapter 17

Karen was in a bad place, but Megan's call to say she was coming for a visit. It seemed like an answer to prayer!

At the airport, Karen checked to make sure the flight was on time. After picking up a coffee, she waited for the plane to arrive.

Mark called and suggested dinner later that week. She agreed and checked her watch again.

She saw Megan walking through the crowd of people. They hurried to meet each other. Sensing the need for friendship, they hugged and hurried off to the car.

The conversation was light on the way back from the airport. It was not time to get into anything deeper.

Later sitting with a glass of wine Karen told Megan what had transpired with Ronan.

Shock and anger was all her friend could offer. "Why would he out and out lie to you? That doesn't make sense."

Megan was struggling to help her best friend. "This calls for serious measures. I don't understand why this man lied to you. Obviously he is not worth your care or attention."

The doorbell interrupted them. A delivery boy brought an armful of flowers.

The PLAN

Karen opened the card: *To you and your best friend—enjoy!* They were from Mark.

What a lovely gesture.

Karen had already told Megan about Mark, but she felt disconnected romantically. Was she wrong about him?

Cari dropped in for lunch and a quick visit. They chatted and laughed about old times. Karen had not said anything about her dilemma to her daughter, and it wasn't mentioned.

"I am a bit worried about your mother," Megan whispered. "She seems to be in a hurry to get into a relationship."

"I agree. Let's watch for problems."

After lunch, Cari promised to bring Josh over to meet her Mom's best friend. She hugged them and hurried back to her clinic.

Karen asked Megan if she would like to drive up to Carmel for shopping and dinner. It sounded good, and they finished up and left.

The day was perfect for a drive—early summer sun, great scenery, and the waves on the ocean. It was a majestic sight.

Karen already felt better. The drive always alleviated the stress of the day—and having Megan beside her was a benefit.

The girls wandered through the little stores, laughing and sharing their thoughts. The time flew by.

"I want to take you to the store where I bought my lamps," Karen said as she ushered her friend through the door.

"I love this little village." Megan sighed. "I wish I was closer. We could do this every week."

"I agree. I guess we better head back."

On the drive, Megan brought up the strange situation with Ronan. Somehow the hurt didn't seem so bad. Was that good sign?

Karen was excited for the rest of Megan's visit. She decided to put Ronan out of her mind.

The two friends took the dogs for long walks. Megan had run into Jen and the children a number of times, and they mentioned how much they missed Grandma.

They would be coming down once the children were out of school. Karen looked forward to the two weeks with her son and his family.

The time seemed to fly by there was so much she wanted to share with her friend and their days and nights went on endlessly.

Megan's vacation was almost over, and Mark was taking them to dinner. Karen was looking forward to the meeting. She was anxious to hear what her best friend thought of him.

The girls drove into the city to meet for dinner. Mark made reservations at one of the nicest restaurants. The hostess took them to their table and told them that their guest was on his way.

Mark walked in and headed to their table. After brief introductions, they ordered wine. They chatted about Megan's job in Chicago and some interesting legal issues he was working on.

After dinner, they headed to Fisherman's Wharf. The street was busy with tourists and locals. The sky was full of stars, and the evening turned out to be perfect.

Mark walked them to the car and headed home.

As soon as they were alone, Megan expressed her delight with him and the evening. "What is holding you back? I saw how you two engaged in conversation. You seem like a natural pair."

"I know, Megan. I am just afraid to take the big step. Look how wrong I was with Graham—and then Ronan." Karen sighed.

The week ended end all too quickly. On the way to the airport, Megan was quiet.

"Are you okay?" Karen asked.

"I am going to miss you—and I think you should really take Mark seriously."

"I agree."

They hugged and said good-bye.

Karen's cell brought her back from her thoughts. Cari wanted to come over with Josh for dinner.

"Of course. Is everything all right?"

Cari laughed and promised that everything was good.

Chapter 18

Karen decided to stop in the city to pick up some necessities for dinner. She hesitated when she saw the lady from the card reading coming toward her. They exchanged greetings.

"I see you are about to hear some great news. Enjoy," the woman said and went on her way.

Driving home, Karen couldn't stop thinking about the chance encounter. She walked in the door and was surrounded by the dogs. She was glad to be back. She walked to the computer to check for an email from a client. Lynn invited her to dinner on Sunday. Mark would be there too. Smiling, she returned a positive reply.

Cari and Josh walked in; they looked like they were going to burst.

"What is going on here?" Karen asked.

Carissa giggled and held out her left hand.

Karen was thrilled to see a beautiful diamond ring.

The engagement was a big surprise for Cari, but they loved each other so much.

Josh had taken her to meet his parents.

"They really liked me, Mom—and you will like them too."

They told Karen all the plans for the wedding. Josh would like to get married at his family home in the next year—if that was okay with everyone.

Karen just wanted them to be happy. "I am fine with whatever."

The wonderful evening came to a close, and they headed off. Karen was smiling and planning for the big event.

Summer brought warm days and long evenings. Tyler and his family would be arriving soon. He promised not to tell anyone in Chicago about the engagement. Karen was planning a party when they arrived.

Mark was in her life a lot more, and she felt at peace with this. They were actually planning the engagement party together. She was hoping to include neighbors, friends, and family.

Josh and Cari took Karen to meet his parents. There was so much to arrange, and meeting them was such a pleasure.

Cari had been right. Josh's family was so nice and loved her daughter. That part of her life was falling nicely into place.

Karen made another trip to the airport to pick up Tyler and the family.

Her home was filled with children. Their first night was a family dinner with Cari, Josh, and Mark. There was a round of introductions and squeals of delight when Jen noticed the ring.

Everyone was getting along. Laughter and good times filled the air.

Lynn and Rob dropped in to meet everyone.

Tyler pulled his mom aside. "I really like your friends, especially Mark."

Karen smiled and gave her son a hug.

Cari and Jen were talking about the wedding and insisting that the children would be part of the big day. Kennedy wanted to know what her dress would be like, and Ethan seemed totally oblivious to the female chatter. He wanted to play with the dogs.

The evening came to a pleasant close, and everyone drifted off to bed.

Tyler came back downstairs to sit and chat with his mom. "Tell me about your life here, Mom."

"Actually, I am really happy here. My decorating business is booming, and Cari is so happy.

Tyler smiled. "You always thought of us first, Mom."

Before they knew it, they were both yawning. She gave her son a hug and kiss before heading to bed.

The PLAN

The days were busy. She even took the family to see Carmel. Each day was filled with a new adventure, and then there was the upcoming engagement party. There was so much to do.

Finally, the day arrived. As the guests arrived, there was excitement in the air. Over cocktails, Tyler made a heartfelt speech to his sister and her fiancé.

Everyone was so happy. It was how Karen had envisioned her life.

She got the buffet ready for her guests. Everything looked perfect. Her hard work had paid off.

Mark was constantly at her side, helping and making sure everyone was looked after. He smiled, and she blew him a kiss.

All too soon, Tyler and family were heading home. The two weeks had flew by. She gave Jen and the children big hugs. She took Tyler aside and said, "Look after your family, my dear. I love you so much."

She told everyone she loved them, and they boarded the plane. Karen felt alone. Since she was already in the city, she called Mark to see if he would like to meet for dinner.

After agreeing on a location, she decided to shop for a while.

In one of her favorite boutiques, she thought about Ronan. He had called a number of times, but she had ignored the calls. The pain wasn't there anymore—just anger.

Everyone really liked Mark, and Karen was happy with him. He was genuine and caring. He had changed so much since they first met—and all for the best.

She picked up a book he wanted. They had not seen each other for a couple days. He had thought she had enough to do with her family. He knew there would be lots of time when they left.

Dinner was perfect. Out of the blue, Mark asked her if she would like to go to Santa Cruz for a couple days. He had a client there and had a meeting with them.

She could have Cari and Josh stay at the house for the dogs, and she and Mark would leave the next day. They called the evening early and headed home to pack.

Is this a good idea? I've made enough bad decisions lately. She went ahead with the planned trip. Heading to bed, she finally felt at peace.

Chapter 19

In the morning, she felt a sense of excitement and adventure. She took the dogs for a long walk. She stopped to chat with Lynn and Rob. They were heading to the city for a day of shopping.

The day passed quickly. Cari would be over after work, and Karen checked the final details of her suitcase. Mark pulled into the driveway, and they were off.

The drive along the coast was breathtaking. Mark had planned the best route. They arrived at the hotel before dinner and explored the scenic area.

In the hotel bar, they stopped in for a glass of wine. The mood was warm, and Karen felt a definite tug at her heart when they exchanged glances. *Is there hope?*

Dinner was pleasant, and they headed to their room. They were tired after the full day. Mark got his papers ready for the meeting, and Karen decided to get ready for bed.

They chatted and drifted off to sleep.

Mark was up early for his meeting. He ordered room service and told Karen he would be back later in the afternoon. She made plans to enjoy her day.

She called Cari to ask about Clinton and Moxy.

"Mom, they are dogs. They are fine. Josh is working from your house today. Stop worrying."

Karen got dressed and picked up a brochure in the lobby. She headed out on her adventure. Santa Cruz was a beautiful city. The ocean and mountains made it unique and inviting. Many art displays added to the beauty.

The morning passed quickly. She stopped at a little bistro for lunch. The lobster bisque was so good. In a wine store, she picked up a nice bottle of wine and two glasses. It was time to see what her true feelings were.

She checked out some of the local restaurants. She wanted to find a romantic place for a quiet dinner. She found one that overlooked the water. She went ahead and made reservations.

Mark arrived shortly, and they discussed his meeting. Karen told him about dinner. He was pleased that she had taken the step. They got ready for their evening.

They decided to take a walk and look at some of the local points of interest. She felt him reach for her hand, and all seemed right with the world. They wandered around the city and headed for the restaurant. It was all she had hoped for: the views were amazing, and the food was some of the best she had eaten. Mark was relaxed, and she noticed a side of him that she had failed to notice before—and she liked it.

They held hands and strolled back to the hotel. Karen mentioned the wine, and they went back to their room to enjoy the rest of the evening. She realized how good she felt. Everything seemed so right.

She felt relaxed and warm. Mark's arm encircled her, which was what she wanted. They were lost in their passion, and he unzipped her dress. Her body took over, and he made her feel like she had not felt in years.

When she awoke, Mark was sleeping soundly with his arm over her. The night had been wonderful, and Karen felt like a new person. He stirred and smiled at her. Once again, they made love.

They spent the day sightseeing, shopping, and enjoying each other. Mark had a final meeting in the afternoon. Afterward, they would have dinner and relax. He found a place for dinner and dancing and was looking forward to the night.

Back in their room, after a wonderful evening their passion once again took over.

Mark was a perfect lover, patient, loving and attentive everything Graham had lacked.

Karen and Mark had become a special couple, and it was obvious to their friends and family. Looking back, she was so glad she had accompanied him to Santa Cruz.

Thanksgiving was just around the corner. She decided to invite the family and some friends. She loved the planning and cooking. Tyler, Jen, and the kids were going to fly down. Cari and Josh would be there too. Josh's parents would be there too.

She would do all her shopping in the city and then give herself a couple of days to get everything organized. Since Mark would be in court, she would have lunch alone or give Margaret a call since they hadn't met since the summer.

She ran from store to store. She loved the hustle and bustle of the season. Thanksgiving was always an important holiday, and this year, it was even more important. She had so much to be thankful for.

Karen called Margaret and set a time for lunch. She picked up Thanksgiving decorations before lunch. She loved shopping in the city.

She found a handmade dollhouse. She knew would be a hit with her granddaughter, and there was a wooden speedboat Ethan would play with for hours.

Margaret waved from the table at the café, and Karen headed over. They chatted about life, house sales, and decorating adventures. After lunch, they parted ways, promising to meet before Christmas.

On her drive home, her thoughts went to Christmas. *What a change from last year—and I hope it will get even better!* It would be her first Thanksgiving in her new home. She would be surrounded by family, new friends, and the hopes for a wonderful future.

The PLAN

She stopped at the market to pick up some flowers and a little gift for the children. The thought of everyone being around brought a smile to her face.

When she got home, the children were already playing with the dogs. Tyler and Jen were full of questions, and excitement filled the air.

Looking back, there were regrets, but she had a feeling a whole new world awaited her. *That is what I plan to concentrate on. Now is the time to truly reflect on the meaning of Thanksgiving and enjoy family.*

Her home was full of family and friends. They were enjoying the season, and love and happiness filled the room.

Chapter 20

The aroma of turkey, pumpkin, and spices wafted through the house. Mark poured wine for the guests. Laughter and happy voices filled the air.

There certainly is a lot to celebrate this year.

The children asked so many questions about Thanksgiving and how it started. Cari and Josh decided to take them and the dogs for a walk prior to dinner. The table was set, and all they had to do was sit down when they returned.

Dinner was festive. Everyone seemed to enjoy themselves. After dinner, Mark decided to go home and come back for breakfast.

Tyler and Jen settled the children into bed and then came back to chat with Karen before turning in. They were leaving the following afternoon. It was nice to have some alone time with them. They asked Karen about Mark.

She smiled and told them she was very attracted to him, but it was nothing too serious.

Tyler laughed and mentioned how Mark looked at her.

In the morning, Karen made breakfast. Mark brought a large bag of warm bagels. At the kitchen table, they discussed baseball, school, and life.

Tyler packed the rental car, and they headed for the airport.

The PLAN

Karen noticed that Mark was tense. She wondered what was wrong.

He looked at her, took her hand, and produced a small box from his pocket. Looking deep into her eyes, he asked, "Will you marry me?"

The moment seemed to last forever. She felt tears run down her cheek, and she said, "Yes!"

"I love you, Karen. You are so special to me."

She did love Mark. She had been afraid to admit it to anyone, including herself.

He had thought of everything. He went to the car and came back with a bottle of champagne.

"I love you, Mark. You have made this the best holiday ever."

They curled up on the couch, toasted each other, and enjoyed the day.

Tyler called to tell her they were home safely. Not wanting to wait, she told him the news. He was thrilled by the great news.

Cari was thrilled too—but not surprised.

Karen took Mark's hand, and they headed upstairs.

Before Christmas, dinner parties and social events filled their time. Mark was spending more and more time at the house. He still wanted to get married before he officially moved in. She loved his old-fashioned values.

Josh and Cari were going to his parents' house for Christmas. Karen and Mark were invited, but they declined. Mark had made plans for the two of them once he knew the family would not be home. He was keeping them a secret though.

On Christmas Eve, Cari and Josh came over for dinner. When they left, they asked if they could take the dogs. Josh's parents lived in the country, and they would have lots of places to run.

Mark handed her an envelope. Inside, there were two tickets to Paris. "Christmas in the most romantic city!" She was thrilled.

They arrived in Paris on Christmas afternoon. Mark had thought of everything. When they arrived at the hotel, there was a small Christmas tree in their room. Chocolates and wine awaited them.

"Karen, you have changed my life in such a wonderful way. I can hardly wait till you are my wife.

She took his hand and led him to the window. They looked out over the beautiful city and the Christmas lights.

They spent their days at galleries and designer stores.

Mark laughed, "We couldn't be in Paris and miss the shopping."

Once the holidays were over, they flew back to be home for New Year's Eve. Karen had never been happier.

Lynn and Rob were having a party.

The coming year held many promising events and future joy for all of them. It was a new beginning.

Looking back on the year, so much had transpired. There were disappointments, and there was joy. The good times far outweighed the bad times. Confusion and apprehension had turned to knowing and following the path of love and understanding.

After a year of turmoil, tears, and joy, life was on the perfect road to happiness.

Karen had been given the wedding date for Cari and Josh. May was a lovely time of year. There were so many plans to be made. It was going to be fun and hectic.

Megan was coming down for a visit. She would love to help. They made plans for the visit, the shopping excursions, the dress, the flowers, and the menu. Karen looked down at her ring. It sparkled almost as much as her mood.

The three months before the wedding were filled with events. With dress fittings and parties, the time flew by.

The invitations went out. The catering was in place. The flowers were picked. It was a constant rush. It was so nice to have Mark bring her down to the peaceful world of the two of them enjoying each other's company.

Karen had seldom felt the peace and contentment she had when she was with Mark. Looking back, she had never thought it was possible.

The last ten years had been her personal hell, but she had never given up hope that there was something out there. She had a comfortable home in her favorite city. She was surrounded by friends and family. Looking toward the sky, she smiled and said, "Thank you. The plan is finally coming together."

The PLAN

There was so much to do. Cari and Karen went to the city to look for dresses. They picked out two specialty stores that carried enough styles so they could find her gown.

The million-dollar question had not been asked. Would Cari ask her father to give her away? The question had been burning in Karen's head, but she didn't want to bring it up with her daughter. She didn't know why, but it had not been discussed. She hoped seeing Graham again would not bring back all the pain and frustration. She would ask Cari in the morning. *I might as well get it over with.*

Karen called her daughter, and they planned to have lunch in the city. They would compare notes and see what was left to do.

They arrived at the same time.

"Cari, are you going to ask your father to give you away?"

"Mom, you won't believe this. I called him to tell him about my engagement. He really didn't seem interested. Last week, I called to tell him about the wedding. He apologized and told me he would be in Europe on business—and he couldn't cancel."

Karen saw the tears in her daughter's eyes. "Cari, we will all be with you. And because it is your day, you decide how you want to handle this."

Karen was pleased he wasn't coming—and she was not surprised. How many times had he missed graduations, birthdays, and special occasions because of work?

Cari reminded her mom that she still had things to do. After a long lunch, they hugged and went their separate ways.

Karen decided to get some things taken care of and hurried off to the first store.

"I can't believe it is you!"

Without turning around, Karen knew it was Ronan. A sickening feeling came over her as she turned around.

"I guess it is a small world," she answered. "I am just heading to an appointment. You will have to excuse me." She felt his eyes on her back as she hurried away. *I can't believe this is happening.* The old doubts and pain returned, and she stopped. *There is only one way to go forward.*

Turning around, she headed back toward Ronan. He was coming out of the coffee shop. "Do you have a moment?" she called.

"My time is in your hands."

"There is a little park down the street. Let's go there."

They sat down on a bench. Karen felt a surge of strength run through her. "Ronan, I really need to know why you had to lie to me about your wife and family."

He looked away.

She could see his anger. *Is it from being caught?*

"Yes, Karen. I lied, and I am sorry. I was—and am—going through a bad time. You were such a bright and warm light in my life in the dark times. I didn't want to lose you."

"I left a thirty-five year marriage to someone just like you. Don't think I am foolish enough to become part of your ongoing problems. I just need you to know I am not interested." She stood up.

Ronan reached out a hand to stop her, but she was already gone—physically and mentally. He looked beaten, and she wasn't at all sad about it.

Her pace picked up, and she felt good. *Enough lies. My future looks even better than before.*

In the cake store, her spirits lifted. There were so many options. She knew what Cari wanted and had been instructed to make sure it was not a typical wedding cake. *That could be interesting.*

The friendly clerk asked Karen to sit down to discuss the possibilities.

"Cari's favorite is carrot cake, and Josh loves chocolate. Can you do that?"

"We could do a bottom layer of carrot and then add a layer of chocolate. Why don't I come up with some ideas and drawings, and you and your daughter can come back in a couple of days."

"That is great. Here is my number. Call me when you have the plans."

She went to find something to wear for the big day and Mark called. They made plans for dinner.

With a couple of weeks to go, everything was falling into place. Karen had been so busy that she had little time to think about

The PLAN

anything but the wedding. She developed a wonderful relationship with Josh's parents, and they were always in and out of each other's homes.

Megan arrived from Chicago, and another pair of hands was a welcome addition.

This is so exciting. I have always dreamed of Cari's wedding. And now she is actually living the hustle and bustle of the plans.

The dress was chosen, the gifts for the attendants were ordered, and their dresses were purchased.

Mark offered to pick up Tyler, Jen, and the children at the airport.

Cari and Josh found a wonderful minister to do the honors. It seemed like nothing could go wrong.

Chapter 21

The weather was perfect, and Karen went to the market to get the finishing touches. She had picked flowers from the yard and arranged everything to match the wedding party. Gathering momentum, she hurried from store to store. She was so happy.

Cari's best friend from Chicago was the maid of honor. Two girls from work and Jen were the bridesmaids, and Kennedy was the flower girl. Ethan was ring bearer.

Mark was making sure everything was ready in the yard.

The gifts for the attendants were carefully wrapped and placed on the tables. The candles were ready to be lit. It all looked perfect.

The house was filled with friends and family. After running around and doing what needed to be done, Karen felt at peace with the world.

Her cell rang. "Hi, Mom. I hope you are not going to be upset, but I just got a call from Dad. He cut his trip short to come."

She caught her breath before she answered. "I am so happy for you, dear. I know you wanted him there for you."

"Mom, you are the best."

Karen's old cold anger kept welling up. She actually felt ill. *This is ridiculous. Will he be here tonight or not?*

Guests started arriving, and a party mood engulfed the night. Dinner was served, and speeches were made. Everyone was happy—and the night was drawing to a close—when Graham's car pulled into the driveway.

Cari was so excited and made all the necessary introductions. Tyler and the family didn't seem too impressed.

Graham gave Karen a kiss on the cheek and told her how wonderful she looked. She felt nothing but betrayal.

The evening went well. Kennedy and Ethan had been entertaining everyone with their antics. Cari and Josh were having a good conversation with Graham.

Why am I feeling so intimidated by him? Karen wanted everything to be the way they had envisioned—a happy time for all.

She assumed that Graham would stay at a hotel, but Cari was taking him home with her. *Is he alone? I hope he didn't bring his mistress.*

When she first saw Graham, there was nothing. *You need to face your demons and get past them.*

Cari said, "Mom, thanks so much for a wonderful evening. I can't imagine not having you a big part of my day."

She exchanged notes with Josh's parents about what still had to be done. She snuggled against Mark. He felt comfortable and warm. He was definitely what she needed. *Now more than ever, I realize how lucky I am.*

When the last guest left, Mark pulled her close. Everything else was unimportant. She could get through the big day—and she would.

Mark kissed her and promised to come over as soon as he got out of court.

Tyler and Jen headed upstairs. *It is so wonderful to have them all here.*

"Megan, let's just sit and have a tea." They curled up on the couch and discussed the evening.

In the morning, Karen called Josh's Mother to see if she needed any help. They all had coffee together. She really liked them, and they had a beautiful old home with a large yard where Cari would marry the man she loved.

"We are so happy that we could have the wedding here," Carol said.

The wedding was only a couple of days away, and they all wanted perfect weather—and for it to be a day to remember.

Karen excused herself and headed home to make dinner for the family. Since Megan was already getting dinner ready, Karen decided to give the dogs some fun time.

Mark arrived, and they chatted over a glass of wine.

He said, "I can understand how Cari would want her father here, but how are you?"

"I am fine. And if it makes Cari's day, I am all for it."

After dinner, Megan helped clean up, and they headed to bed.

Tyler, Jen, and the children went shopping and sightseeing. Mark would be in court all day. Karen and Megan would run the final errands together. She called Carol to make sure there was nothing they had forgotten.

The dresses were at Karen's house. The girls would get ready there and then take the half-hour drive to the country home where the ceremony would take place.

Appointments had been made for hair and makeup. Megan would be at Cari's side to ensure that everything the bride needed would be handled without any stress.

Excitement was in the air, and Karen felt good. Her only question was if Graham brought his mistress. Since Cari was staying there, she would find out from her daughter.

Stop all the negative thoughts. Who cares who he brings? On second thought, I won't bring it up with her.

Karen realized it was time to head home to get ready.

Megan was wonderful. Dinner was cooking. Cari, Jen, and the children were having a good time. It was girl's night—even Tyler was shipped off to spend time with the groom. Everyone had a great time. Megan made a moving speech about the past and remembering warm times when Cari was growing up.

Mark called and said, "Hi Karen. How is the girl's night going?"

"All is well. I am looking forward to tomorrow."

Karen and Megan sat down for a chat and a glass of wine. The house was quiet.

The PLAN

They awoke to beautiful sunshine and clear skies. Excitement filled the air.

Breakfast was made, but no one was interested in eating. The house was alive, and everyone was happy and excited.

The hustle and bustle was invigorating and kept out any negative thoughts Karen had. The next eight or ten hours would be spent with Graham—and whoever he chose to accompany him.

Cari was a so stressed that it seemed to cast a shadow over the day.

"Calm down, my dear," Karen said.

"I know, Mom. I have waited so long for this day. I just want it to be perfect."

Megan made tea, and the ladies worked on her hair and nails.

It is going to be fine. It has to be for my best friend and my family.

When it was time to leave, tears welled up in Karen's eyes. Cari was a vision of beauty; the dress and flowers were perfect.

The driver took the bride and her attendants. Megan and Karen had left earlier. A beautiful and happy day was unfolding.

Karen cried when Kennedy and Ethan led the bridal party. Seeing Cari and her father coming down the path was very emotional.

Everything went as planned. They were husband and wife. The speeches and dinner were wonderful. Graham was alone and chose to have Megan at his side.

Wandering through the guests, Karen felt at ease with Mark at her side. Watching the bride and groom dance to their favorite song brought back memories for Karen.

Graham tapped her shoulder and said, "Can I have this dance?"

She hesitated, but since it was Cari's day, she said yes.

The music and being in Graham's arms were too much for her. As soon as the music ended, she excused herself and went to find her friends.

When the bride and groom left for their honeymoon, the guests prepared to head out.

Chapter 22

After bringing Tyler and his family to the airport, Karen was happy to find that Megan had made lunch for the two of them. They went over the details of the wedding and agreed it had been a success.

"Megan, I don't understand my feelings toward Graham. When we danced, I almost felt like it was meant to be."

"You were caught up in the moment."

The gals decided to go for one last drive to Carmel before Megan left. The afternoon tea and scones were wonderful.

That evening Mark took them to dinner at their favorite place.

Dinner and the company were warm and inviting. Everyone shared details of the past few days.

After wine and idle chatter they all decided to part for the evening.

Mark reminding Karen, "Let's get together tomorrow."

Megan would be missed when she left.

They drove home, and Karen said, "Let's sit and have wine. It is our last night together."

The dogs were at their feet, and the world seemed at peace. Remembering times from the past, they laughed and made plans to get together in the fall.

The PLAN

That night, Karen tossed and turned.

After breakfast, they headed to the airport. Watching the plane taxi down the runway, Karen felt a moment of loss. At home, the sadness was still there. Was it Megan leaving or something else that was bothering her?

After walking the dogs, she checked her e-mail. Cari and Josh were having a great time and were so happy. Karen was pleased. *Another chapter in her life put to rest. I know they'll be happy. They seem perfect together.*

Graham called and said, "Karen, I wanted to thank you for making me feel welcome in your home."

"Why are you calling? I thought you would be happy to be back in Chicago and busy at work."

"When I was out on the West Coast, I realized I had made a lot of mistakes. I was so impressed by how you handled everything while I was there. You know you could have made it very difficult."

"Graham, it was not the time or place to make anyone feel out of place or unwanted."

"Thanks again and take care of yourself."

Karen felt a sense of sadness, and tears trickled down her cheek. *Why is this so hard to let go of?*

Years flooded back into her mind, and she searched for a reason for this change of attitude. Clinton and Moxy had other ideas and pushed their noses into her lap. Bending down to give each a hug, she headed to the kitchen. It was time for a tea and a treat for her loyal buddies.

Mark called to say he would be a little late.

"Why don't we get together tomorrow night?"

"That would be great—if you are okay with it."

I really need some time on my own—and even this one night might help. Time to get comfy and prepare for a quiet night.

She made tea and wondered why the confusing thoughts kept haunting her. Graham—and what he had done—repulsed her. For the past ten years, she had expected nothing. As it turned out, she was not disappointed.

Why did she start to question her feelings? Was it just the wedding and the family being together? Was it the right time, the right setting, and the wrong feelings?

In the morning, she felt better. An appointment in the city gave her the break she needed.

After her meeting, she decided on a walk to shake any negative thoughts from her mind.

The ocean seemed so peaceful. *I just want peace and happiness. Why can't I accept things they way they are?*

A strange sense of calmness came over her. She started breathing deeply.

Out of nowhere, a voice said, "We keep running into each other. I see you are still troubled." The little lady from the card store took her hand and looked at Karen. "I told you there are bridges to cross. Take your time. In the end, it will be wonderful."

The woman disappeared into the throng of people, leaving Karen alone.

A warm feeling pulsed through her, and she felt better. *Patience will prevail, and all will be well.*

She decided to invite Mark to a casual dinner. He promised to be over by seven.

In the driveway, Karen looked at her perfect home. Her family was settled, and Graham was in the past. She decided the plan had all come together. The future looked promising, and she would make it the best she could.

About the Book

Karen has lived a life filled with accomplishment and happiness, but it's time to start over. She's exhausted from a lifelong fight with her own emotions and dreams. After all, she believes, it's never too late to start over.

For more than thirty-five years, she has been married to Graham, but it just isn't enough. She has her marriage, her children, and her career. He has his career. But when she starts to doubt his fidelity, she knows it's time to make her own decisions. With the children grown and living their own lives, Karen envies them that freedom, that sense of raw possibility, that sheer wonder at what the next day will bring.

When it's time to start her next chapter, she holds her head high—her heart pounding with excitement and a bit of fear—as she leaves her stagnant life behind and set her sights squarely on the future.

San Francisco has always been her dream city, and now she will make it her own. With a tremor of excitement, she makes her move, with no idea what awaits her or how her life will change.

This will be the journey of a lifetime: a rollercoaster of emotions, shocking revelations, tears, and laughter.

About the Author

Isabel Morrow wanted to write a book for a long time. After raising two wonderful children, having a career, and looking after a home, the time seemed right. With the publication of The Plan, she has accomplished a major life goal.